Finding Hope
By Elizabeth Diaz

Book 1 in the Generations of Hope Series

Finding Hope

Finding Hope
Written by Elizabeth Diaz
© 2015 published by Elizabeth Diaz

Cover design & Formatting done by Leah Banicki

Find Elizabeth Diaz online:
https://elizabethdiazauthor.com

Facebook:
https://www.facebook.com/ElizabethDiazAuthor

All rights reserved solely by the author. The author guarantees all contents are original and do not infringe upon the legal rights of any other person or work. No part of this book may be reproduced in any form without the permission of the author.

Disclaimer: This is a work of fiction. Any resemblance of characters to actual persons, living or dead, is purely coincidental. The author holds exclusive rights to this work.

Elizabeth Diaz

For Joel David Wing
January 22, 1984 – June 26, 1984

Finding Hope

Chapter 1

August 1978

Nineteen-year-old Olivia Martinelli backed away from the front door of their brick home when she heard the sound of her parents arguing. They lived at the end of a quiet cul-de-sac a few miles outside the city. The lawn was neatly mowed, several beautiful flower beds surrounded the house, and a shallow creek gently flowed through their backyard. If you drove by, you'd never guess the unpleasantness that waited inside.

Olivia decided to check the mail and go sit by the creek in the backyard until they finished their argument. She trudged to her favorite spot, a small bridge Papa had built for the neighborhood children to play on when they were younger. They had spent hours pretending to sail the oceans or cross the bridge to an imaginary land with princesses and dragons.

Olivia looked around to make sure no one could see her, then kicked her shoes into the grass and slipped off her nylons. She sat on the edge of the wooden bridge and dipped her toes into the creek. The cool water rushed over her feet. The sight of the birds competing for the sunflower seeds in the feeder helped her to relax. She had hoped
to talk with Mama about her plans to move into her own apartment, but it seemed every time she tried to bring it up something went wrong.

Last week, when they sat at the table to play Yahtzee, Mama had her coffee and they chatted about work. Olivia thought it was the perfect time but, before she had the chance to tell her, the phone rang. It was Mama's office. Someone had made a mistake and needed her to come back in to help straighten things out. A few weeks before, it had been a friend of Mama's that had stopped

Finding Hope

by unannounced for a visit, and today she and Papa fought. Olivia had to tell her soon, but she knew the news would upset her.

With suppertime approaching, Olivia decided to head back to the house. Mama was at the stove when she walked in, and the savory aroma told her it was pork chop night. Olivia set her purse, shoes and nylons in her room and rejoined Mama in the kitchen. She washed her hands and pulled three plates from the china hutch. She balanced the glasses and silverware on top of the plates and walked to the dining room to set the table.

"Olivia, how many times do I have to tell you not to stack the dishes on top of each other? Make two trips and that way you won't break anything." Mama's razor sharp tone was familiar to Olivia. The constant criticism over each decision she made had caused Olivia to doubt her ability to make *any* choices in her life-- even the minor ones. Olivia acquiesced and there was no more talk until it was time to eat.

Dinner was a silent affair. Mama sat at one end of the oval table and Papa at the other. Olivia sat in the middle, which is where she often found herself during their arguments. She hurried through the meal as fast as she could and escaped back to the sanctuary of her bedroom.

That night, Olivia pulled her luggage out from under her bed to pack up some of her belongings for the move. A quick glance around the room revealed there wasn't much to take: clothes, a few books, and the framed picture of she and Mama on Papa's lap taken Christmas morning last year. Olivia had few pictures of all three of them, and this one was by far her favorite.

Christmas was one of the few happy times at their house because Mama seemed to come alive. She spent evenings and weekends baking while Christmas records played in the background. She shopped and hid gifts throughout the house. Mama loved getting dressed up for the fancy parties she and Papa attended and often paused under the mistletoe for a kiss on their way out the door. If only Mama could be that happy all year.

Olivia folded most of her clothes and packed them first, followed by a few of her photo albums and favorite cassettes. She filled her suitcases and slid them back under the bed. It surprised her how most of her belongings and a lifetime of memories could fit into a few suitcases.

Sleep was slow to come that night because this was the first time she'd gone against Mama's wishes. Mama had made decisions for Olivia throughout her life, from the length of her hair to the color of her bedroom walls. For the most part it hadn't been a problem. Olivia wanted to please her and was eager to go along with whatever she demanded. But now it was time to grow up and stand on her own two feet. Olivia was scared.

As usual, she awoke to the sound of cabinet doors being slammed as Mama muttered under her breath. It had always been this way, and Olivia never understood what made her Mama so angry at life. Anytime she tried to ask Papa why, he remained silent.

Olivia dressed, brushed her long black hair, and put on her lip gloss. The only thing to do before she left for work was to eat breakfast. She sighed and reminded herself that soon the uncomfortable meals shared with her parents would be a thing of the past. At the ceramic tiled counter, she watched the toaster while Papa buried his head in the Glenn Haven Daily News. Olivia poured herself a cup of Earl Grey tea and buttered her toast. She breathed a sigh of relief when her friend, Eric, pulled into the driveway to pick her up for work. She kissed Papa's cheek and murmured a good-bye to Mama, then hurried out the door to Eric's rusty pick-up truck.

"Good morning, Sunshine. Eric's limo at your service."

Olivia grinned at her friend. He had made mornings bright ever since they were kids at the bus stop. "I don't think too many people would ride in this limo," she teased. She cleared the crumpled lunch sacks, an apple core, and three Doobie Brothers cassettes off the seat.

"Hey, I wasn't done with that!" Eric joked as Olivia reached to toss the apple core out the window. The easy banter they shared was how Olivia imagined it would be if she'd had a brother. By the time they pulled up to the office, Olivia had shaken the tension that seemed to follow anyone who visited the Martinelli house.

Olivia walked up the cobblestone sidewalk while Eric parked. What was once a charming bungalow home had been converted into an Insurance Agency. Cheerful yellow and purple petunias added to the home-like feel. She reached in her purse for the key to unlock the old wooden door and begin the day.

The office hummed to life as Olivia flipped on lights and opened the blinds. Her desk was situated by the staircase and faced the front door. She was receptionist and secretary to the business owner, Zig Orban, who was a friend of Eric's dad.

Olivia gathered the files Zig needed to do interviews. He planned to hire another salesman, and several candidates would be there later that morning. Zig arrived mid-morning on most days after making a few client contacts, which was a good thing because she needed time to prepare. He was a great boss but was like a tornado: loud, always in a rush, and leaving messes wherever he landed.

Soon the office was a hubbub of activity. The bell above the door chimed when a man walked in and approached her desk. She glanced at him while she finished a phone call. He seemed to be a few years older than her and was average looking.

Olivia hung up the phone. "What can I do for you, Sir?" She scribbled a note in shorthand as she spoke, then put it in her tray.

"I'm Jake Raines. I'm here to interview for a sales position." Olivia's thoughts were wavering a bit: *Well, maybe not so average looking after all. He has an amazing smile.*

"Mr. Orban is ready to see you. I'll take you back now." She led him to the conference room and tapped on the door.

"Come in!" Zig's voice was loud enough for someone in the offices across the street to hear.

Olivia smiled at the incredulous look that crossed Jake's face. Most people responded the same because Zig was a character. His booming voice was the tip of the iceberg. He was tall with a heavy frame, and his eyes sparkled with mischief. He was an incredible businessman with a heart of gold.

"He's loud but harmless," Olivia whispered before she opened the door and ushered him in. "This is Jake Raines. He's here for his interview."

Jake reached to shake hands with Zig, and they seated themselves at the table. "Is there anything else you need, Mr. Orban?"

"No, we're fine, Olivia. Thank you." She slipped out and later repeated the process with two other candidates before she left to meet a friend for lunch.

Olivia and her best friend, Nora, met weekly at Flo's, a little diner down the street from the office and near the bank where Nora was a teller. When you first walked in, you saw a long counter with several red-cushioned bar stools and a cash register from days long ago. The floor had small black and white checkered tiles. There were four booths along the wall with cushions that matched the barstools. Each table held an ashtray, salt and pepper shakers that could use a wipe down, and coffee mugs with "Flo's Diner" printed on them.

"Hey Olivia!" shouted Madge, the restaurant's sole waitress.

"Hi Madge," Olivia greeted as she joined Nora in their usual booth. Madge's grin revealed the large gap between her front teeth. She returned to the animated conversation she was in the middle of with another customer.

Madge had worked in the diner for the past thirty years. Her daddy owned it before her, and after he passed away, he left it to her and her husband Hank. She often seated herself with the customers to catch up on the local gossip. It was normal to hear Hank yell through the little window that separated the kitchen from the the dining room, "Get up and bring me the customer's orders!" Somehow it all worked, and the regulars adored them.

"How were the interviews today?" Nora asked as Olivia settled into the well-worn seats of the booth.

"I think they went well. Zig interviewed three guys. He spent the most time with the first man who came in. I imagine that's who he'll hire. I'm sure I'll know soon because Zig isn't one to procrastinate."

Nora dropped the menu and grabbed Olivia's hand. "Oh, I forgot to tell you! Mr. Depoy called and said we can stop by for the key. The tenant moved out a few days ahead of schedule, and the apartment is ready. Do you have time to come with me tonight?"

"Of course!" Olivia exclaimed. "Meet me at the office after work and we can walk over." The girls finished their lunches and shouted good-byes to Hank and Madge.

Chapter 2

It was a beautiful summer evening. There weren't too many more to enjoy with fall around the corner. Olivia and Nora strolled up the tree-lined avenue after work, and they were pleased to find the landlord at the house making repairs.

Mr. Depoy was near bald with small round spectacles. He had thrown his tweed jacket on the ground beside him, and his shirt sleeves were rolled up above his elbows. His dress pants had dirt smudged on the knees. Olivia thought he resembled a professor more than a handyman.

Mr. Depoy glanced up. "You can go on upstairs and check things out while I finish up with this porch railing." He nodded to the front door, so Nora and Olivia walked up the steps.

The door flew open before they could turn the knob. A woman stood there in nothing but a shiny gold bikini, her long white hair twisted into a tight bun. She was tall and thin and had to be at least seventy-years-old.

Olivia stepped back, unsure of how to proceed, but Nora always knew what to say. "Love the suit. I'm Nora." The woman gave them a curtsy.

"Elva Fields, but you can call me Miss Elva. I couldn't help but overhear you girls talking to Timmy about the empty apartment. I'm glad Mr. Henson moved out. He was a grump." With that she turned and walked away, leaving Olivia and Nora alone on the porch. They glanced at each other and tried not to giggle.

Mr. Depoy finished the railing. "Well, you've met Mrs. Fields. Are you sure you still want the apartment?"

"She'll be sure to keep us entertained!" Nora piped up and Olivia nodded in agreement.

"Take a peek around. I'll be up in ten minutes or so. Mrs. Fields' cat got on the roof again."

Olivia and Nora chuckled. Anyone so kind to such an eccentric woman had to be a sweet man. They soon saw him climb up his ladder and come back down with a fluffy white cat.

They heard Miss Elva exclaim, "Giselle, my poor baby!" as they climbed the stairs.

It was nothing fancy. Each room had been freshened up with a new coat of paint. It had two tiny bedrooms with cramped closets, a bathroom you'd be lucky to fit one person in, and a kitchen with a one basin sink. The stove and fridge seemed to be from the 1950's. The living room was unremarkable, other than a large four-paned window that faced the quiet street with an amazing view of the river. That was what excited Olivia most about the apartment. The river was her favorite place in town.

After they filled out the lease and paid a security deposit and first month's rent, Mr. Depoy gave them a set of keys. Olivia and Nora danced around the unit after he left. "I can't believe we did it!" Olivia gazed in wonder at the keys she held. This was the beginning of a new life.

Nora grabbed Olivia by the shoulders and brought her back to reality. "Yeah, now all that's left is to tell your parents." That put a damper on her spirits. Olivia forced herself to go home. She wished she could move out without a run-in with Mama.

By Friday night Olivia was a nervous wreck. *I wish I were braver like Nora. Nora wouldn't be bothered by Mama's sharp tongue and constant criticism.* Olivia was sensitive and timid. She knew that contributed to some of her relationship problems with Mama and hoped by moving out she would show Mama, and herself, that she was an adult; an adult who could make her own choices and take care of herself.

Olivia packed the last of her things and lay awake most of the night thinking about her plan for the morning. When she awoke Mama was talking to herself downstairs. Olivia was on pins and needles waiting for Mama to leave for the grocery store. Papa was in his workshop, his favorite place to relax. Working with wood was a hobby that consumed much of his time. Typically, he wouldn't come back upstairs until late afternoon.

After she heard the car drive away, Olivia's hands shook while she dialed Nora's number to tell her the coast was clear. She left a carefully-written letter for Mama and Papa on the table. It was the coward's way out, but she hadn't been able to gather enough courage to tell Mama in person. She stood outside and waited for Nora to pick her up. When Nora pulled in with her brother's car, they threw her suitcases in the back seat and took off.

Olivia was free. No more need to tiptoe around or worry about what mood Mama might be in when she got home. No more angry tirades from Mama about Papa's many faults.

She couldn't imagine what it would be like to go through a whole day without criticism from her mother. Olivia and Papa didn't argue, but she often wished he would stand up for her. He spent the bulk of his time in his recliner or downstairs in the shop.

Olivia was quiet most of the car ride to the apartment, but Nora made up for it by chattering about her plans. It helped Olivia loosen up, and soon she began to pitch in her own ideas.

"Let's think of what we need to get settled." Olivia began a list on the back of an envelope she'd found in her purse. "It'd be nice to have beds." They couldn't help but laugh because they had their bedding, but no beds--small detail. It was going to be an adventure for sure!

"My mom offered the beds from my and Allen's old rooms, since we're both moved out now. I'm sure she'll let us use the dressers, too." Nora was lucky. Olivia not so much.

"I have nothing to contribute. Mama will be furious when she finds out I'm gone." Olivia moaned as she thought of the confrontation that was soon to come.

"It's okay, Olivia. We'll find what we need. When Allen and Jen bought their house, they got all kinds of hand-me-downs. I'm sure once our friends find out what we need, they'll pass things our way. We'll be fine."

Olivia couldn't wait to try their new touchtone phone. It was so much faster than the rotary phone at home. She decided to call her Nonna to let her know she'd moved out and give her the phone number to their apartment.

Nonna answered her phone in a few rings, and her comforting voice was like balm to Olivia's nerves. "I thought it may happen this way. Your Mama does love you, and she's tried to protect you from all the hard things in life that could come your way. She's terrified of your life being as hard as hers."

"Mama has a hard life because she chooses to make it that way." Olivia never could understand why Mama was so unhappy.

Nonna was silent a moment. "I know it's been tough at home. I wish she hadn't been so harsh with you, and sometimes I think some of it is my fault. Nonno was such a strict disciplinarian, and I never interfered with his ways. Back then it was the norm. Now I see how we could've handled things in a different manner."

"You'd think she'd be different if she hated it so much. I would never be as critical as she is to me if I had kids."

"It's a hard cycle to break, *Tesoro*. She is easier on you than Nonno was on her. He didn't just use words to get his point across."

Olivia and Nonna grew quiet. It was a hard topic to discuss, and they didn't bring it up often. She and Nonna talked a while longer and made plans for Olivia to fly down to New Orleans and visit in a few months for Thanksgiving. They hung up and Olivia wondered what she'd have ever done if she didn't have her Nonna to talk to.

She and Nora decided to sleep in the living room their first night. They giggled as they made beds on the floor and ate supper off paper plates. Most of the night was spent talking about all the fun things they could do, now that they didn't have to report to anyone. They could come and go as they pleased, sleep as late as they liked on the weekends, and listen to whatever they wanted to on the radio. Although Nora had a much better relationship with her parents than Olivia did, she was also excited for the freedom that came with being on her own.

Sunday morning they "shopped" in Nora's parent's basement and found some mismatched silverware, a few chipped plates, and some odds and ends for the kitchen. They laughed and talked while sorting through the boxes. Several hours later they trudged back home, arms laden with supplies to stock the apartment. The adventure had begun.

Chapter 3

The first day of school was something Brad Parks looked forward to each year. The tall brick building was ready to welcome its students on this crisp fall Monday morning. The windows gleamed, the grass had been mowed in neat lines, and the flag seemed to beckon all to enter. The sound of his footsteps echoed in the empty hallways as he unlocked the door and walked into his classroom. Brad flipped on the lights and began to write on the board:

Mr. Parks
Latin 101 1st Declension Endings
-a   -ae
-ae   -arum
-ae   -is
-am   -as
-a   -is

This was his third year teaching at Glenn Haven, and he loved it. He glanced up as his friend, Ben, stopped by his classroom. "Hey, Ben, how's it going?"
"Alright. Are you ready to tackle another year of Latin with the freshmen?" Ben asked.
"I can't wait!" Brad would have never dreamed he'd become a Latin teacher. In college he had taken a Latin class on a whim and ended up switching his plans from teaching high school English to this ancient Italic language.
His Latin professor had recommended him to Glenn Haven, and he was hired not long after graduation. He moved to the small Michigan town three-and-a-half years ago. He met Ben Grant and his wife Lisa at church his first month in town, and they hit it off

from the start. Brad spent many weekends at their house, and they became his closest friends.

The shrill sound of the bell interrupted their conversation. Ben saluted him before he headed back to his own classroom. Brad stood at his door and watched as the halls filled with students. Their voices carried through the hallway, locker doors slammed and the final bell rang. The kids hustled into their classrooms and found their seats.

Brad took a deep breath and met their expectant gazes. "Welcome to my class. I'm Mr. Parks, and I am excited to introduce you to the fascinating language of Latin."

Tuesday morning at work Olivia received a letter from Mama. She was hesitant to open it, but knew her mother deserved to be heard. Eric plopped in the chair next to her desk.

"What's wrong?" he asked, when he saw her eyes fill with tears.

"I got a letter from Mama. She's disappointed in me. She stressed that if I'm adult enough to move out, I should be adult enough to talk to her and Papa face to face. I knew I couldn't though, Eric. She would get angry and I would have backed down again. I needed to get out."

"It's going to be okay, Olivia. They knew this day would come. Your mom knows you're a good girl with a good head on your shoulders." He gave her a quick hug before he had to get back to work. "I have a lot to do before I train Jake next week. I'm happy for you, Olivia. You are going to be fine, and someday you and your mom will get past this."

When Olivia arrived home that evening there was a pot of hearty beef and vegetable stew simmering on the stove and the delicious scent of garlic bread wafted from the oven. Nora was a great cook. She had helped her mom in the kitchen since she was a little girl. Olivia set the table as she told Nora about Mama's letter.

"You should've seen it, Nora. You'd think I was twelve-years-old and had run away. She's sure we'll end up pregnant or someone will murder us. I wish we could talk things out, but you can't talk to her!" Nora listened in sympathy.

"Olivia, you made the right choice. You *must* believe that. Your mom *is* impossible to talk to once her mind is set. I think doing it this way was the most practical decision."

They talked a while longer and then heard a knock at the door followed by a cheerful, "Yoo-hoo, it's Elva Fields from downstairs. There's a wonderful aroma coming from your place and I thought I'd join you!"

Olivia opened the door and there she was: this time in a pink bikini with blue polka dots and a bright purple bathrobe thrown over it. In her hand she held a mason jar filled with questionable looking brown liquid. She pressed the jar into Olivia's hand and walked into the kitchen. Olivia couldn't tell what was in the jar and was afraid ask.

Elva sat down while Olivia set another spot at the table and placed a steaming bowl of stew in front of her. "What's in the jar, Miss Elva?" Nora's curiosity got the best of her, and Olivia stifled a laugh.

"It's my homemade vanilla. You put a couple vanilla beans in a jar, fill it the rest of the way with vodka, and let it set a few months. Keep it away from direct sunlight, too. You've never smelled anything so marvelous in your life! Even if you don't have vanilla beans it's okay. I like it with just the vodka."

Elva winked before she took a bite of the soup. Olivia and Nora couldn't help but laugh and Miss Elva joined in.

Miss Elva sparked some lively conversation while she finished her soup and then waltzed out, leaving the dishes for the girls. When the door shut Olivia and Nora collapsed in laughter. Miss Elva was going to be a trip.

Chapter 4

"Good morning," Pastor Malone greeted the congregation. "I'm Pastor Dave, and I have a few announcements to make before we get started."

Sharon Jenkins sat in the pew by herself. She had attended Glenn Haven Baptist for a few months now. A college friend had told her that the best way to land a man in a small town like this was to find one at church. She hadn't attended since she was a little girl, but figured she could do whatever it took to find a husband. She had hoped to be married before she graduated from college and hadn't planned on using her teaching degree at all. Although there had been no shortage of dates none of them lead to a serious relationship.

"Here are a couple prayer requests and a praise to add to our list this morning before we pray," Pastor Dave began.

She was unsure the first week if she wanted to give up one of her treasured weekend mornings to go to church, but the minute Brad drove up in that dark blue 1977 Camaro she decided it couldn't hurt to stick around a while. Whoever owned a car like that must be well off, and that was at the top of her wish list for a husband. Her interest had piqued when he got out of the car. He was tall with a strong build. He had dark wavy hair and gorgeous green eyes. He even had dimples when he smiled! She was ecstatic when she noted he had no ring on his left hand.

"Please turn in your Bibles to Philippians chapter four," Pastor Dave announced.

The first few weeks she hung back and observed. She saw he had a lot of friends and the respect of those he interacted with. He seemed to spend a lot of time with the same couple, so she sought out the wife and introduced herself. Each week she had feigned interest in whatever Lisa had to say.

Today she was rewarded for her efforts with an invitation to their house this Sunday for lunch. Sharon knew Brad often joined them there after church as well. It was the perfect way to make a casual introduction! She tapped her foot as she waited for the pastor to wrap up his message so she could get to the enjoyable part of the day.

Brad perched on a stool that was off to the side of the pulpit. He strummed his guitar while Pastor Dave finished the service with a prayer. After the final "Amen", he put his guitar in its case and weaved through the aisles to find Ben and Lisa.

"Great worship today, Brad." Lisa was a tiny brunette who struggled to hang on to her son's hand while holding her squirming daughter in the other arm. She had no luck though. As soon as he heard Brad's name, four year-old James charged towards him. Brad grinned and gave him a high-five and tugged on two year-old Nicole's ponytail.

"These kids wiggle more than newborn puppies!" Lisa sounded exasperated. Ben found them before the kids escaped again, took Nicole into his arms, and helped his wife corral James so they could head home.

Brad walked out with them to their car. "So, what are you guys doing this afternoon?"

"You know that you don't have to hint for an invitation. You're always welcome at our house for lunch. I invited a few others today, too." Lisa's voice was muffled while she bent over to buckle the kids into the dark brown station wagon.

Brad laughed because it was a bit of a game. If he stayed around long enough after church, Lisa took pity on him and invited him to eat with them. He knew she'd ask, but he had perfected the starving single man face in case she forgot.

Lisa was a great cook. She and Ben loved to host the singles and young married couples in their home. Even though their home wasn't spacious, their door was always open and Brad spent a lot of time there.

"Is there anything I can pick up from the store for you?" Brad asked.

Lisa thought for a minute, "If you don't mind, I forgot to get ice for the drinks and I could use a few more chairs. Would you mind loading six from the fellowship hall for me to borrow?"

"Sure, no problem." Brad headed back into the church to get the chairs.

After making a trip to the store, Brad pulled up to their Cape Cod house. The sound of laughter could be heard through the open windows. The mouth-watering aroma of homemade yeast rolls reached him before he opened the cheerful red door.

The women were in the kitchen, and most of the guys helped Ben put together a makeshift table that everyone could fit around. Their dining room had a table for four, but several couples had brought card tables and chairs to add on.

Once they were all together, Lisa threw a long tablecloth over to make it look like one table. The white walls were covered with pictures of the children and Ben and Lisa's families. The scuffed wooden floor was in need of refinishing, but it was a happy home and Ben and Lisa were warm people who had the gift of hospitality.

The women bumped into each other in the cramped kitchen as they dished up the potatoes and carrots and put the warm rolls in baskets. Lisa sliced the roast and asked Sharon to stir the pan of brown gravy that simmered on the stove. Sharon could see into the dining room while she stirred and kept a subtle eye on Brad. She saw how quick he was to lend a hand and how sweet he was with the kids. The more she saw, the more determined she was to have him. Her strategy was working well so far.

Soon it was time to find a place to sit so they could eat. Sharon tried not to appear too eager to take the seat by Brad. She gave him a shy look. "Is it okay if I sit next to you?"

"Sure, no problem. This seat's all yours." Brad stood to pull the chair out for her. She sat down and they chatted while they waited for Lisa to bring out the salt and pepper.

Ben cleared his throat when his wife took her seat. "Alright, let's pray and then we can dig in." He bowed his head and everyone around the table followed suit. After the prayer, Lisa began to pass the food around the table. Brad grabbed a roll and handed the basket to Sharon. When their eyes met, he couldn't help but admire how beautiful she was. Sharon had taken great care to look her best. She was a beautiful woman and knew it. She had her blonde hair cut in the same style as Farrah Fawcett. Her blue eyes were dusted with eye shadow that made them appear ever more luminous. Her light blue pantsuit accentuated her trim figure. She was pleased he had noticed her at long last.

Ben entertained them with stories of the kids' latest escapades. The funniest was when James and Nicole had to sit in the church service with Lisa because the nursery was in the middle of a renovation. It happened to be a week Pastor Dave was on vacation, and he had asked Ben to preach in his place. Every so often James would clap followed by an enthusiastic "That's my daddy!" Lisa had tried to quiet him, but he was thrilled to be in with the grown-ups and watch his daddy preach.

The afternoon passed with pleasant conversation and much laughter. When Brad got up to head home, Sharon gathered her things as well. "Hold on Sharon." Lisa put her hand on her arm. Sharon grew frustrated when she saw Brad get into his car and drive away. She had hoped to talk to him outside. They had talked a little during the meal, but she wanted more time with him.

She turned back to Lisa. It was obvious Brad was close with this family, and they would tell him if she was rude. "What's up?" Sharon tried to appear as if the interruption wasn't a problem.

"I wanted to make sure you knew we host a Bible Study here on Tuesday nights. We'd love to have you join us."

"Oh, thank you so much. I'd love to come. I'm so glad I found a group that's serious about their faith." Sharon knew the words it would take. Her sister was a "Jesus Freak" and that's all she ever talked about. At least she could put those countless hours of listening to Jill to use. It might help her get close to Brad, and that was what she wanted.

Tuesday night Sharon hoped she arrived ahead of the others. She wanted to make sure she got a seat next to Brad. He was well-liked, and she had a feeling she wasn't alone in her admiration of him. Lucky for her, she was by far the prettiest (at least compared to the women she'd met so far). Tonight she wore her bellbottom jeans and an adorable striped blouse.

Lisa met her at the door. "Hey Sharon, I'm glad you're early! The kids have been *crazy* today. Would you start the coffee for me while I get them in bed?"

Sharon spied Brad in the living room. "No problem, Lisa. Is there anything else I can do to help?" she offered loud enough for Brad to hear. She wanted him to see how accommodating she was.

"That should be it. I'll be down in a few minutes." Lisa picked up James and headed up the stairs to put him *back* in bed.

Sharon made the coffee and poured a cup for Brad and added some creamer. She knew exactly how he drank it from the dinner earlier that week. "Here Brad, I poured a cup for you so you can drink it before you start the lesson."

"Thanks Sharon." He took a sip and nodded approvingly. "How's the school year going so far?"

She slid into the chair next to him. "It's been great. I'm so glad I found this group. It's a lifesaver for someone new in town. I was so nervous that I wouldn't meet anyone my age when I moved here. I was thrilled when I found your church and there were so many young families."

"Well, we have something in common." It hadn't been that long since he'd been new in Glenn Haven. He listened to Sharon as she talked about her teaching job. He was reluctant to end the conversation, but it was time to get started.

After Bible study, Brad retreated out to the porch. It was one of his favorite places to sit. It was a full moon, and the air had started to turn colder at night. Ben and Lisa were busy with a couple that had come for the first time, and the single girls were tidying up the kitchen to help Lisa. Brad enjoyed the quiet and the beauty of the night sky.

Sharon saw him go out and dried her hands on the dish towel. She planned to sneak out of the kitchen and join him. Hope, another girl in their group, tied on an apron and reached for the dishcloth Sharon had been using. "I can finish the dishes, Sharon.

You go visit." She took her place at the sink, and Sharon joined Brad on the porch.

"Oh, hey Brad. I didn't know you were out here. Do you mind if I join you?" Sharon feigned surprise that he was on the porch.

"Of course not. Here take this chair." Brad got up and moved to the other side of the porch. They talked about school most of the time. They had a lot in common since they were both teachers. Brad glanced at his watch in surprise. "It's eleven!" He couldn't believe the time had passed so fast.

Sharon stood up. "Oh my goodness, I had no idea it was that late. I need to get going. I have a room full of first graders that have lots of energy to face in the morning." She congratulated herself as she walked to her car. She could feel him watching her leave. Things had progressed as she'd hoped. She was on his radar.

Brad thought about their conversation on his way home. He liked her. *Maybe I'll ask her to go for coffee sometime.* He knew if he found someone Lisa would be thrilled. She wanted her friend to be as happy as she and Ben were.

The next morning Brad met Ben in his classroom before school started. They had made a habit of meeting to pray. "So, what's going on with you and Sharon? Lisa was so excited when she realized you two were out on the porch. I had trouble keeping her inside."

Brad laughed, "I don't know. She seems pretty nice, and we have quite a bit in common. I think I'm going to ask her out."

"What? You mean Mr. High Standards himself has finally found someone who qualifies?" Ben often teased him about his reluctance to date because he always found something that he didn't agree with about a woman, often before giving her a chance. "That gives us something to pray about for sure. Let's do that right now before time gets away from us." After they prayed, Brad decided he would ask her out the next time he saw her. He wanted to get to know her better.

Chapter 5

Olivia arrived at the office a few minutes earlier than usual Monday morning. It seemed so quiet now. Before she had moved, Olivia and Eric rode in to work together. Now that she lived closer to the office, she was often the first to arrive. Zig needed her to gather materials for him to go over with Jake. Zig had decided to hire him and orientation started this week.

The first thing new hires had to learn was how to pronounce and spell Zig's name. He was Hungarian, and it was an unusual name: Szilagyi Orban. He told people to call him Zig, but on legal documents it had to be spelled out. He was great with people, and selling insurance policies came easy to him. He leaned on Olivia, though, to do most of the paperwork.

Last week she had prepared all the documents Zig needed to go over with Jake, so all that was left to be done was place the folders on the conference room table. She filled a pitcher of ice water and started the coffee; then loaded a tray with coffee mugs, styrofoam cups, and cream and sugar packets. She opened the curtains in the back of the room to let in the light and put a cup of pens in the center of the table. After the conference room was set up, Olivia hustled back to her desk to greet clients.

Jake arrived fifteen minutes early, so Olivia seated him in the reception area. He glanced over at her with interest. "How long have you worked here?"

"It will be a year in September, and I love my job. Zig is a fun boss and one of my best friends works here too." Olivia couldn't help thinking to herself how cute Jake was. He was about 5' 10" with brown hair and dark brown eyes. He had an average build, but what stood out to her was his smile. He seemed like a happy person. She had heard him and Zig laugh often during his interview. "Are you new to the area?" Olivia was curious to learn more about him.

Jake looked uncomfortable for a moment. "Yeah, I moved here from Iowa. I worked in sales there too, so I was glad when I found the ad in the paper. I love to work with people."

"Well, you'll do great here then. That's what makes a salesman." Olivia smiled in encouragement.

"It'll be nice to make some friends because I haven't met too many people since I moved. I'm glad I found work. I wasn't sure how long it would take." Olivia agreed and thought about how difficult it would be to start a new job in a town where you didn't know anyone. She guessed it wouldn't take Jake long to make friends. He already seemed at ease in the office, even though he had just met them last week.

Zig charged in the front door like a tornado and whisked Jake away. Olivia turned her attention back to the sizeable pile of paperwork on her desk. She was thankful for her fast typing skills and the IBM Selectric she had to work on. It was so much better than the typewriter she learned on in high school. She spent the rest of the morning putting policies together, transcribing her shorthand notes, and entering premium payments in the ledger book. The morning flew by and before long it was time to meet Nora at Flo's Diner.

The walk downtown was the highlight of Olivia's day. She loved being outside. Today was sunny with a gentle breeze, green leaves had turned crimson and yellow, and the crisp air had the smell of fall. She inhaled and strolled to the restaurant. Madge seated her in no time. For once she had arrived before Nora. Olivia glanced around and noticed Jake by himself several tables away. He grinned and came over to her table. "Why don't you join me, there's no point to both of us eating alone."

"I'm waiting for my room mate. You're welcome to join us though. There's plenty of space." They waved Madge down to let her know Jake had switched tables.

"Who's this?" Madge asked while she set another placemat and cup at the table.

"This is Jake. He started at the office today and is new in town," Olivia explained, hopeful that Madge wouldn't embarrass her.

"Lucky you. He's handsome. I sure wouldn't mind staring at that face all day." Jake grinned and Olivia blushed, unsure of what sort of response was expected.

"Madge, stop yer yackin' and get back here with the orders," Hank yelled from the back. "People don't want to wait all day!"

Madge huffed and scurried back to the kitchen.

Jake leaned back in the booth, and Olivia tried not to be distracted by his playful smile. "Do you eat here every day?"

"No, my roommate Nora and I meet a few times a week though. It's my favorite place. It's been here since my mama was a little girl."

Olivia glanced up when Nora approached the booth. "Scooch in and introduce me to your boyfriend." Olivia blushed and scooted over. Between Nora and Madge she'd never be able to look Jake in the eye again.

"Nora, this is Jake, a new co-worker. Jake, this is my roommate, Nora. She's a pain."

Nora threw her head back and laughed. They ate and talked, learning more about Jake and his move to Glenn Haven. Nora might be a pain, but she kept the conversation from growing awkward. By the end of the meal Olivia felt more comfortable with Jake, and she wasn't nervous about what to say on their walk back to the office.

They passed by Olivia's apartment on the way back to work. She spotted Miss Elva on a ladder washing her front windows in yet another bikini, this time she had a sweater on over it. Olivia couldn't pass by without saying hello.

Miss Elva hustled down from the ladder. "Introduce me to your young man, Olivia. He sure is a dish!"

"He's not my young man, Miss Elva. He's a *co-worker*. He moved to the area a few weeks ago and joined Nora and me for lunch."

Miss Elva reached out to shake his hand. "Elva Fields, former ballerina and neighbor to Olivia and Nora."

Jake bowed down and kissed her hand. "Jake Raines, and it's an honor Miss Elva." Miss Elva nodded in approval.

"Well, get on with you both. I need to finish these windows." With that she hustled back to the ladder. Jake raised his eyebrows and Olivia stifled a laugh.

"There's got to be a story behind that woman!" Jake held his laughter until they got out of earshot.

Olivia laughed with him. "We moved in last week, and so far she's had a bikini on whenever we've seen her. We're wondering what she'll wear when it starts to snow. That was the first I'd heard about her being a ballerina. Who would have known? She shows up to eat with us every few days and always makes us laugh. She keeps things interesting!"

When they arrived back at the office, Jake held the door open and Olivia walked through. Eric was returning at the same time. When he saw them come in together, he gave her a sly wink. Olivia rolled her eyes and sat down.

Jake cleared his throat. "I enjoyed lunch. Thanks for letting me sit with you and Nora. I hope we can do it again soon."

"You're welcome to join us anytime." Olivia fiddled with a few files on her desk, unsure of what else to say.

As soon as Jake returned to his desk, Eric poked his head out of his office. "Is it clear to come out?" She knew he would tease her when he saw them walk in together.

"Yes! He was at Flo's when Nora and I were, so we invited him to sit with us." Eric took his usual spot next to her desk and pestered her until she made him get back to work. He was like a protective big brother. *Maybe being an only child wasn't all that bad,* she thought.

That evening Olivia called Nonna to make plans for her visit to New Orleans. They decided which airline she'd use and then chatted for a while. They hung up, and Olivia filled the sink with soap and water so she could wash the supper dishes. She and Nora had decided Nora would cook and Olivia would clean up. Olivia's mom had never taught her to cook but expected her to do most of the household chores. They thought this arrangement would be best for the time being.

When the last dish was dried and put away, she went in search of Nora. She was nowhere to be found inside, so Olivia peeked out the window. There she was, sitting on the front porch laughing with Miss Elva – Miss Elva with a purple bathrobe over her bikini, tall and lean. Her head held erect as she sat gracefully next to Nora.

Nora was average height and a little chubby, with wild red hair. She was forever trying some new product to tame the curls, but they had a mind of their own. She had a much more adventurous sense of fashion than Olivia. Today she had on a blue t-shirt with a floor length tie-dye skirt she had made. Her hair was pulled back in a ponytail, and she wore large feathered earrings.

Olivia took the opportunity to enjoy the quiet and flipped through a *Better Homes and Gardens* magazine. Her eyes were drawn to an article on decorating. She wondered if they were allowed to paint in the apartment.

She grabbed the phone and called Mr. Depoy. He told her it would be okay to paint the walls, but not to touch the wooden trim. When they moved out, it all had to be painted back to white or they'd lose their deposit. Olivia wouldn't have dreamed of painting over the beautiful cherry trim and agreed to Mr. Depoy's terms. She was sure they'd be there for years, and she wanted to make it their own.

By the time Nora came back inside, Olivia had several colors picked out from the magazine and showed them to her. "I called Mr. Depoy to see if we can paint and he said yes! What do you think?"

"It doesn't matter to me at all what color you choose: purple, red, green. Go for it! Just no polka dots or stripes. And don't ask Miss Elva's opinion! I can't *imagine* what her apartment looks like."

"Purple? Really?" Olivia spent the rest of the evening folding pages in the magazine that had ideas she liked.

Finding Hope

By Friday, Olivia had begun to miss Papa. She decided to visit her parents the next morning. Nora asked if she wanted company, but Olivia knew she had to face Mama and Papa alone at some point. Nora breathed a sigh of relief. Even *she* was intimidated by Mrs. Martinelli.

When dawn arrived, Olivia lay in bed as she watched her curtains sway in the breeze. Mama never liked the windows open. She didn't want the house to get dusty. As a result, the air always seemed stale at home. She got up and nibbled on her usual tea and toast. It was pure bliss to sit in quiet without all the tension between Mama and Papa permeating the room.

Eric had agreed to drop Olivia off at her parent's house on his way to his favorite hobby: fishing at nearby Lake Chapin. Papa wasn't upstairs, so she wandered downstairs to his shop. He looked up in surprise and grinned. "There's my girl!" He hugged her tight and kissed her cheek.

"Hi Papa. I've missed you so much." He sat on his old metal stool and Olivia climbed onto the wooden one next to him, just as she had since she was a little girl. They would chat about whatever came to her mind while she watched him create model airplanes that flew, toys that would delight any child, and wind chimes that even Mama loved.

Today Papa was painting a birdhouse. She had loved being in the shop with him and preferred the cool temperature of the basement over the frosty atmosphere upstairs with Mama. The scent of pine and fresh paint filled the room. His tools hung on a pegboard with a long workbench stretched around the perimeter of the room, covered with projects he was working on. He was happy here.

She told him all about her new apartment and her spunky neighbor, Miss Elva. Papa told her about the craft show he had in a few weeks, and they caught up while the morning puttered along. Once in a while Olivia lent him a hand, cleaning his paintbrush or helping him choose paint colors.

When she heard the garage door open and Mama's car pull in, she began to have second thoughts. Why on earth had she come?

She should've allowed Mama a little more time to cool off before she tried to talk to her. Papa recognized the expression on her face.

"You're going to have to talk to her sometime, Olivia. You might as well go on up." She knew it would be something she had to do alone, since Papa avoided confrontation with Mama at all costs. She climbed the stairs still unsure of what she could say to appease Mama.

Olivia found her in the kitchen and watched as she put the groceries away. "Hi Mama." She hoped a soft tone might soothe her mother's bruised spirit. Mama turned and eyed her, and for a moment Olivia thought she was ready to forgive her.

"I wondered when you'd get the nerve to show up and talk to me like an adult." Mama's words were often used as a weapon, and she was an excellent marksman.

"I'm sorry, Mama. I should have talked to you before I left. I knew you wouldn't agree, and I didn't want to fight." Mama harrumphed and continued on with her chore. Olivia wanted to help, to somehow cross the barrier between them, but the kitchen was Mama's domain. She had made that crystal clear since Olivia was a young girl. Olivia would sometimes ask to help make dinner or learn to bake, even as a teenager. Mama always shooed her away as if she were a pest. She preferred a brisk pace in the culinary department so she could sit and rest after a full day at work.

Olivia sighed. Once again she had been unable to have a real conversation with Mama. "I wanted to see you and Papa. I've missed you." Mama didn't respond. Olivia decided it was useless to try and make peace and scampered back downstairs to say goodbye to Papa. He packed up a box that had paint brushes and all the paint supplies she'd need to work on the apartment. He then offered to drive her back home. She gladly accepted since she didn't want to wait on Eric to return.

Olivia was thankful she had a project to throw herself into when she got home. She worked on the living room and hallway first. As she painted the soft green over the stark white walls, the

Finding Hope

room was transformed into a warm, inviting place. She admired her work and couldn't wait for Nora to get home from visiting her parents to see the end result. Nora loved it and was impressed with how short of a time it had taken Olivia to finish. She asked Olivia to do her bedroom, too.

"I didn't think it would matter, Olivia, but now it feels so homey." Olivia made a list of other things she wanted to buy when they had the money. She decided to measure the couch. She was sure with Nonna's help she could figure out how to make a couch cover. She snapped a few pictures with her Polaroid to show Nonna when she flew down to New Orleans to visit her at Thanksgiving.

Monday morning was quiet at the office because Zig, Eric, and Jake were at a sales meeting. Olivia took the opportunity to turn on the radio and do the odd cleaning jobs that were often neglected. The janitor emptied waste baskets, vacuumed and cleaned the restroom. Other than that, if Olivia didn't do it, it didn't get done. She took a few hours each month during the sales meeting to dust, clean the windows and mirrors and scrub the ring from around the bottom of the coffee pot.

She was in the conference room spraying cleaner on the windows when the guys returned. They found her as the song "Take A Chance on Me" came on the radio. Jake turned it up and began to dance and lip sync the words of Abba's song to Olivia. Zig and Eric shook their heads and exited back to their offices. Olivia couldn't help but laugh. He was crazy! When the song was over, he took a bow and went back to work.

Most days it seemed Jake found one excuse or another to come to the reception area and joke with Olivia. He hadn't asked her out yet, but she knew he would soon. The thought both excited her and made her nervous. She hadn't dated much, and he was several years older than her. Old enough to be ready to settle down. Olivia knew she was getting way ahead of herself, but she enjoyed living with Nora and her newfound freedom was precious. She wasn't sure she was ready to get involved in a relationship.

Over the weekend Olivia made a trip to the local hardware store to find colors for Nora's room. When she walked in, she made a beeline for the paint department. She agonized over which color would suit Nora best. In the end, she chose a deep purple for the walls
and black to paint the furniture. Nora had an exuberant personality and the bold colors would suit her. When she got home and showed Nora the colors, they decided to start painting that afternoon. They took a break at suppertime, and Olivia showed Nora the list of other ideas she had to improve their home.

"Hey! I forgot to tell you, Olivia, there's a new photography studio that opened downtown. I heard the prices aren't too steep. You want to check it out Monday at lunch?"

"Sure!" Olivia had wondered what she would do with their bare walls now that they were painted. After her Monday morning work, she rushed down to the studio as planned to meet Nora. They meandered in and wandered around the shop. The walls were covered with black and white photographs, and they were stunning against the cherry red walls.

Nora pulled her to the one that caught her eye. It was a picture of a concrete stairway leading to a brownstone building. There were several men sitting on the steps with work-stained clothes, cigarettes in hand, enjoying a much-needed break from the demands of menial labor. Nora decided to buy it since it would look amazing on her purple wall.

For the living room, Olivia wanted a nature scene. She wandered to the back of the studio where pictures taken in Glenn Haven were displayed. This room had color prints situated on slate gray walls. She was thrilled when she found a photo of her favorite spot at the river! It captured the towering oak trees with their brilliant display of fall color. Alongside the winding river was the worn bench that often seemed to beckon her to come sit and absorb the surrounding beauty. The photograph mesmerized her. She knew in the cold winter months she could get lost in this picture and imagine she felt the warmth of the autumn sun.

Finding Hope

"All set?" asked a woman behind the cash register who was about ten years older than Olivia and Nora. Olivia nodded and handed her the picture she had chosen. "I'm Hope. I'm so glad you came to check out the studio."

"Your work is beautiful." Olivia didn't know much about art, but the photographs had moved her. "I would love to have this kind of talent." Nora agreed as she handed over her picture to be wrapped.

"It's all God. He created this beauty, and I try to capture it." An uncomfortable silence followed. Olivia and Nora both were weary of the Jesus Movement that had everyone and their brother trying to convert them. Olivia gave a polite nod that she hoped sent the message that she wasn't interested.

"We'll be back. We have an entire apartment to decorate." Nora gave her a wave as they headed out the door to head back to work.

When Olivia returned to her desk, there was a bouquet of wildflowers lying by her typewriter. She glanced around, puzzled, and met Jake's eyes. He winked and then disappeared around the corner to his desk. She headed to the kitchen to hunt for a vase for the flowers.

All day, whenever she glanced up at the flowers, she thought of Jake. He was so funny, but he also had a sweet side. Nora would tease her for weeks if she brought the flowers home, but she wanted to set them on her windowsill.

That night she held her head high when she carried in the bouquet. Nora smirked and returned to chopping chicken for the casserole. While Olivia set the little table with their chipped Corelle dishes, she hummed under her breath. "Oh, Olivia, you've got it bad!" Nora tossed a piece of chicken at her to wake her from her dreamland.

"He's great, Nora. I can't help it. I don't think I'm reading things wrong. I think he likes me."

"I like anyone who makes you happy, Olivia." With all Nora's teasing, she was a great friend who had been with her through thick and thin.

When she woke up the next morning, Olivia tried on four different outfits before she picked out something to wear. As she brushed her hair and pulled the sides into a barrette, Nora peeked in on her before she left for work. "Wow, you're not dressing up for anyone in particular are you?" Olivia pretended she didn't hear her and finished getting ready.

Olivia arrived at the office anxious to see Jake. She wasn't disappointed as he was already there. He had to settle his first claim later that morning, so he was at her desk often to find forms or ask questions. When he leaned over her shoulder, she breathed in his cologne and her heart began to race. She hoped he didn't notice how distracted she was when he came near.

Throughout the afternoon, he'd pop over to her desk and tell her ridiculous jokes. She couldn't help but laugh. Around two o'clock Zig opened his door. "Are you ever going to ask that girl out?" Olivia's face turned red.

Jake grinned, "Well, since you mentioned it, maybe I will." He turned around and got on his knee. "Olivia Martinelli, would you do me the honor of joining me for dinner at Pauley's Pub tonight?"

Olivia rolled her eyes. "Szilagy Orban, go back to your office. I'm not going out with anyone unless it's *his* idea, not yours!" Zig guffawed, and Jake held his hand to his heart as if she'd shot him.

"I guess I'll have to try again," Jake whispered when Zig left to go back to his desk. Olivia heard Eric try to stifle a laugh from the other room. She sighed. Working with all men could be tiresome.

While Nora cooked dinner, Olivia sat on the counter and told her all about her day. "I knew he liked you, Olivia Martinelli. He looks at you like I look at chocolate cake." They both laughed because nothing was more important in the universe to Nora than chocolate cake.

"Do you think I should say yes if he asks me out again? I haven't known him that long. Should I make him wait?"

"Why wait? Olivia, you're nineteen years old. Have some fun!" Nora pushed her off the counter. "You had better set a spot for Miss Elva tonight. She asked what I was making earlier and, when I told her meat loaf, she mentioned it's her favorite." It was no surprise that after the timer buzzed they heard a knock.

"I'll get it. You pour the drinks." *Nora is bossy in the kitchen,* Olivia thought, as she poured the lemonade.

"Hello girls!" Miss Elva's voice had a pleasant, musical sound to it. Olivia loved listening to her. She took the fur coat that was thrust in her hands. They had wondered what Elva would wear as it got colder. Now they knew: Fur -- and pearls, lots of pearls. "I'm starving!"

Nora served her meat loaf, a baked potato and green beans. "Mm mmm!" Miss Elva speared a piece of the meatloaf with her fork and bit down. An expression of surprise flitted across her face. "Oh dear, it seems I forgot to put my teeth back in. Would one of you girls be a dear and run down and get them for me? They're on the table that's next to the door." Olivia avoided eye contact with Nora and smothered a laugh.

Nora jumped. "I need to use the restroom. Would you run down for her, Olivia dear?" Olivia knew Nora had her, so quickly went downstairs to retrieve Miss Elva's teeth.

She had never been in Miss Elva's apartment and was surprised to see pictures covering every inch of the walls. Many were of a ballet company and a beautiful woman, who she assumed to be Miss Elva, dancing in a leotard. Some of the photos appeared to be taken in other countries. One was a laughing Elva under the Eiffel Tower. She must have been an accomplished dancer.

Olivia continued around the room and saw pictures of Miss Elva with a handsome man, his arm around her and a little girl in her lap, sitting in a model T. There were a variety of pictures of them as the child grew older, until she was four or five years old.

Then the pictures stopped. Olivia wondered what had happened to the man and child? She knew she had to get back upstairs with the teeth, but Olivia could have lingered for hours to study the captivating pictures that seemed to tell the story of Miss Elva's life.

When she got to work in the morning, Jake was perched on the office steps. Olivia had expected to be the first to arrive. "Hi, Jake. Do you have an early client meeting?"

"No, I came to talk to you. Can you sit for a minute?" She sat next to him, and her heart hammered in her chest. "I know you thought the other day with Zig was a joke, but I have wanted to ask you out. Would you want to go to Pauley's for dinner Friday night?"

Olivia scrutinized Jake's face to see whether he was serious. He seemed nervous while waiting for her answer. She nodded her head and ended his agony.

"You will?"

"Of course I will, Jake." Olivia was amused by the look of relief that came across his face.

"Okay, why don't I pick you up around 5:30? That way we can both go home and change into something more casual."

"Sounds perfect. I can't wait!" They stood up, unlocked the door and Jake headed to his cubicle. Olivia wished she could call Nora and tell her, but didn't want Jake to overhear and think she was childish.

On Friday, Jake picked her up at 5:30 as promised. "Let's go eat." He held out his hand and she hesitated for a moment. *Oh loosen up, Olivia, and let him take your hand.* The sparks were immediate, and Olivia was certain her heart would never beat at its normal pace again when she was near him. They walked toward Pauley's and talked nonstop the whole way. Jake asked her about where she had attended school and what year she graduated. They laughed when they realized he'd graduated seven years earlier. He told her funny stories about growing up with four brothers, and she couldn't stop asking questions about what life was like with siblings.

Before they knew it, they had passed Pauley's and gone all the way to the river walk. They decided to get a hot chocolate from a vendor and sit outside and talk. They found a swing that overlooked the river and sat down. Not being face-to-face helped Olivia to relax and open up.

When the sun began to fade, they headed back to her apartment. Jake grabbed her hand again and asked if he could take her out once more before the weekend was over. Olivia forgot about her desire to take things slow and agreed. They decided he'd pick her up on Sunday evening and then head to the beach to walk the pier and watch the sunset. It wouldn't be long before it was too cold for the beach.

When Olivia arrived home, she found Nora sitting Indian-style on the floor in their cozy living room. The lamps let off a cheerful glow. Nora had made a bowl of popcorn and bought two bottles of Coke. "Spill it girl," was the first thing Olivia heard as she walked in the door.

"Oh, Nora, he's wonderful. I had so much fun with him! He asked me out again for Sunday night!" Olivia tried not to sound pathetic. It was their first date, and she hadn't expected such a strong connection. Nora sighed and begged for more details. They stayed up for hours to plan Olivia's outfit for the date and to make a menu for the picnic she had promised to bring along.

Sunday night Olivia put on her jeans and a peasant top she had borrowed from Nora. After she put her favorite hoop earrings in, Nora tucked a flower behind her ear. Olivia knew it'd be cool by the water, so she grabbed a jacket. Since she had told Jake she would pack a picnic, Nora made ham salad for sandwiches and Olivia packed pickles, a bag of chips, and some of the cookies she and Nora had made that afternoon.

When she saw Jake pull up, she yelled to Nora that she was leaving. As she walked out to his car, Mrs. Fields popped her head out the door, "In my day a young man always came to the door."

Olivia shrugged her shoulders. Miss Elva was sweet, but it wasn't 1925 anymore.

Jake gave her an appreciative gaze when she got into his Orange 1963 Chevy Impala. It was a thirty-minute drive to the lake, most of it winding through farmlands. He pulled her next to him in the middle seat, and they sang along to the radio.

At the beach, they spread their blanket and set out the picnic basket. Then they decided to walk the shoreline to the pier. Jake was so easy to talk to. Olivia was surprised at how comfortable she felt with him.

When they got to the pier, he turned and kissed her. It happened so quickly that she had no time to consider whether or not it was too soon. He then pulled her up onto the pier. "Race you to the end!" She couldn't help but laugh as he ran down the pier like a wild man. She couldn't remember the last time she had this much fun.

When she got to the end, he patted the spot next to him and she sat down. They hung their legs over the pier and talked while they watched the sunset. "You know, I think you're special, Olivia. I noticed you were different as soon as I started at Zig's. I am so glad you agreed to go out with me." He leaned in to kiss her again, and this time Olivia didn't hesitate to respond.

Nora wasn't there when Olivia returned home, so she changed into her pajamas and washed her face while she waited. As soon as she heard her footsteps in the stairwell, she ran to the door and pulled her inside to tell her about the kiss. Nora squealed in delight. "I can't believe he kissed you on the second date!" Olivia couldn't seem to wipe the smile off her face when she floated to bed later that night.

Nonna called the next night, and Olivia told her all about Jake. Nonna was happy for her but cautioned her to take things slow. "No one ever regrets taking things slow, Olivia. It's when you move too fast that things tend to end in regret." Olivia decided to change the subject and told her some of the new ideas she had to decorate the apartment.

Olivia and Jake ate lunch together every day that week and met for dinner at Pauley's on Friday. They followed Friday dinner with a walk along the river, which was Olivia's favorite thing to do. Each week after that was the same. She shared about her family and how hard it was to grow up in a home with so much criticism and little encouragement or affection from her mother. She shared about her mom and how negative she was and how her dad never spoke up. She also told him about Nonna and how special she was.

He told her about his family and how things could be different in a marriage if there was love and kindness. After a few months, Olivia knew she had fallen in love. Her one concern was that Jake pushed for them to take things further physically.

"It's okay, Olivia. When you know you love me, you won't hesitate," Jake told her. She tried to explain that she did love him, but it was a big step. Jake assured her when her love was real, she'd want to express it to him. Olivia felt conflicted. Maybe she was naive, but she wasn't ready yet. He told her that he loved her so much he was willing to wait.

Chapter 6

Thanksgiving approached, and Olivia headed off to see Nonna. Mama seemed hurt that she wasn't staying home, but what was the point? Her parents would most likely argue, and the rest of the day would be spent in uncomfortable silence. Besides, Jake travelled back to Iowa to see his family.

On the plane, Olivia grew more and more eager to spend the week with Nonna. She hadn't taken a whole week off work since she started with Zig last year. She peered out the window and thought of how different Mama and Nonna were. Nonna was cheerful and fun loving. She never complained and was always interested in whatever Olivia had to say. Olivia couldn't figure out how Nonna had managed to have a daughter like Mama.

When the plane landed in New Orleans, Olivia hurried to baggage claim and searched the crowd with eager eyes for Nonna. When she saw her, she broke into a run. "Nonna!" she shouted to get her attention. Nonna pushed her way through the crowd and took Olivia in her arms. They hugged for a long time.

"You are more beautiful every time I see you, Olivia Marie." Nonna always made her feel so special. Olivia linked arms with her as they sauntered off to find the car. Olivia chattered all the way to the house while Nonna listened with rapt attention.

When they pulled up to Nonna's charming Shotgun home, Olivia sighed in contentment. This was the place where she was loved and cherished. She adored Nonna's home. It was a muted purple color with midnight blue shutters around the tall windows and burgundy wooden door. The white trim on the house complimented the color scheme, and it deepened the purple hues in a beautiful way.

Nonna held open the wrought iron gate while Olivia carried her luggage up the cement steps. She anticipated cool nights on

Finding Hope

Nonna's little porch surrounded by pots of pink geraniums. They would sit on the old rocking chairs Nonna's parents had brought over from Italy, drink sweet tea, and talk for hours. At times, they could hear strains of music coming from the French Quarter. She had so many happy memories here.

"Why don't you get settled in your room, and I'll see about something for us to eat." Olivia unpacked quickly. Nonna may *say* she'll throw something together, but Olivia knew it would be a feast.

While Nonna put the finishing touches on the meal, Olivia enjoyed the antipasto tray. She popped the marinated olives in her mouth and tore pieces off the loaf of homemade ciabatta bread while she chatted with Nonna. She loved mealtime because whenever she visited, Nonna served dinner like they had in the old country. It was one of Olivia's favorite traditions that had, for the most part, been ignored at home by Mama and Papa. Once done with the antipasto, out came *primo*; the first course which was a serving of fettuccine with alfredo sauce. Then *secondo*, the main course. This was a piece of marinated chicken that was so fresh and tender Olivia could have eaten more. She knew there was much more to come, so she decided to pace herself. *Contorno* came next; fresh vegetables from the market. They munched on them while Olivia's favorite was setting up in the fridge: *Dolce!* Often it was a bowl of fruit, but for this special time together Nonna had made her famous tiramisu. It was smooth and creamy and out of this world. Olivia wondered how Italian women stayed trim! She was sure she would be at least one hundred pounds heavier if she had all this delicious food available every day. The meal ended with a cup of espresso.

Olivia insisted on washing dishes after all the work Nonna had put into the meal. They stayed up late to plan their week. "I want to go to the shop first thing tomorrow and explore." Nonna's countenance changed.

"What is it Nonna? Did something happen?"

"No major catastrophe, but I sold the shop. What's left of my inventory is in the back room."

"But why? You loved it so much, and you're gifted at finding rare pieces." Olivia thought of all the summers she'd spent in the shop with Nonna helping collectors find the perfect item to add to their treasure troves. The store had been full of the old, unusual, and many beautiful things: from books, clocks, and tea sets to magnificent period furniture. It was where Olivia had developed her eye for turning the ordinary into something beautiful.

"I want to garden, go to lunch with friends, even travel a little before I'm too old."

"I do understand, Nonna, but I'm surprised. Why didn't you tell us?"

"Oh, you would have worried and tried to come down to help me. You have your own life, and I didn't want to interrupt."

"You would never be an interruption, Nonna!"

Nonna laid her weathered hand on Olivia's cheek, "You're a wonderful granddaughter, Olivia. C'mon, let's go to the back room. I kept a lot of my inventory so you could start your own collection." Nonna showed her where everything was and pointed to a large trunk in the corner of the room. "I want you to fill that thing up; come as often as you like this week and sort through things. Take anything you want." Olivia hugged her, and they began to talk about her apartment and tried to find things that would fit the plan she had.

The next morning, Olivia woke up to the spicy aroma of cinnamon. It had to be Nonna's cinnamon rolls! She joined her in the kitchen where the walls were a cheery yellow and the cabinets were painted cream. Hand hewn wooden planks served as a floor. In front of the sink lay a colorful braided rug on the floor. The table seated two and was adorned with a beautiful hand-stitched tablecloth. The cloth was made from a piece of sky blue fabric with cherries sewn along the border. Nonna's antique tea set was arranged in an artful fashion on an ornate silver tray. Elegant pieces from Nonna's collecting days accented the simple architectural style of the home. A vase here, a Tiffany lamp there; it all made for a delightful contrast. Olivia brewed a pot of tea while Nonna slathered icing on the cinnamon rolls.

When they sat down to eat, Olivia decided to tell Nonna more about Jake. They had been dating a few months and it seemed like he could be the one. Nonna asked some questions. She wasn't as happy for her as Olivia thought she'd be. Olivia knew Nonna was flying up for a visit at Christmas and would meet Jake then. After that, he would win her over himself with his charm and classic good looks. She let the subject drop as they left for a tour of Olivia's favorite plantation, Oak Alley.

Upon arrival, Olivia stepped out of the car and marveled, once again, at the beautiful setting. Fourteen live oaks lined each side of the long drive to the house. The trees were hundreds of years old, and you could sense the history that had taken place here. If Olivia stopped and watched, she could see the ornate carriages and ladies with elegant ball gowns that had graced this spot so many years ago.

Olivia and Nonna toured the grounds first, taking in the simple slave cabins, the original blacksmith shop, and the vibrant plant life. It was a quiet and peaceful place. People spoke in hushed tones as if not to disturb the memories that surrounded them.

The house had twenty-eight pillars, seven on each side, inspired by the majestic trees in front. There was room after room of exquisite furnishings along with pictures of those who had lived in this home. Olivia couldn't fathom what life must have been like for them. She sometimes longed to experience a simpler way of life and thought it must have been wonderful to live here. She found herself a bit downcast as they left. Things were complicated with Mama, and she wondered where her relationship with Jake was headed. She tried to shake it off so she could enjoy Nonna and her beloved New Orleans.

The last day, they made their annual trek to the French Quarter. They wandered the French market, and Olivia bought souvenirs for Nora, Eric and Jake. Nonna was ready for a rest, and so Olivia suggested a break at the *Cafe Du Monde* for beignets and cafe au lait. She loved to watch the beignet makers through the window in back.

The dough traveled through a machine to be flattened, then was cut into squares by a bladed roller. The beignet maker then would pick up several at a time and toss them into the hot oil behind him. Minutes later the mouth watering treats were lifted out and dusted with powdered sugar. Nonna and Olivia ordered two beignets each and sipped their cafe au laits while Olivia watched all that was going on around them.

New Orleans felt like another world to her. It was crowded and noisy and Olivia felt like she could never get enough. There were artists scattered along the streets, some sketching and some painting their colorful surroundings. The heady scent of food filled the air. Street musicians performed jazz that made you want to get up and dance, even if you're feet were sore from walking. The music of the calliope tickled their ears as the Steamboat Natchez cruised up and down the Mississippi River. This place was magical. Even the buildings were from another era.

Olivia and Nonna had a wonderful week together, and they both cried when they had to part at the airport. They knew they would see each other at Christmas, but it would be some time before Olivia would make it back down to spend time alone with Nonna.

Brad and Sharon had been on several dates, and Brad began to get the feeling that Sharon wasn't the right girl for him. He decided to bring it up to Ben to see what he thought. While he waited in his classroom for their prayer time, he wondered if he was being too picky or if there was an issue with Sharon.

Ben sensed Brad's mood when he walked in. "Hey man, is everything alright?"

Brad tried to gather his thoughts before he responded. "I'm not sure Sharon's the one. I do like her, but she wants things to move much faster than I do for one; which I know is normal, but there's other things, too. Have you noticed there doesn't seem to be much depth to her?"

Ben sighed. "Lisa and I have noticed she doesn't seem genuine. We didn't know what to think. You've spent more time with her than we have, but I agree. Something doesn't add up."

"She's fun and beautiful, but I have seen a mean side to her. Not towards me, but sometimes the way she'll treat a waitress or one of the other women at church. I don't want to hurt her, but I don't see this going anywhere."

Ben gave him an apologetic look. "I know we should have brought it up sooner, but there's not one specific thing I can put my finger on. It's more something we *sense*. We didn't want to interfere or say something that would affect our friendship."

"I need to talk with her." Brad tried to reassure himself with this thought: "I'm sure she's noticed our differences, too."

"Well let's pray, bro. God will give you wisdom." After their time in prayer, Brad felt more at peace. He decided he'd talk to her that evening.

Brad called Sharon when he got home from work and asked if she could meet him for coffee at Flo's. She had sounded so happy, he felt guilty knowing he would hurt her.

Once they were seated at the table, he decided it would be best to be straightforward. "Sharon, I've thought a lot about our relationship. I have enjoyed the time we've spent together. I'm sure you've noticed, too, that we're better off as friends than we are dating." He looked at her hopeful that she would understand.

Sharon sat for a moment in silence. She was taken aback. *What a jerk!* She had spent all this time with his friends at his ridiculous church. She had acted like those girls her sister hung out with acted – pious and pure. The whole thing made her sick. What a waste. He was done with her? Oh no, that's what *he* thinks. She was done with *him*. "That's my cue to leave." She stood up and glared at him while she put on her coat.

"I'm so sorry, Sharon. I didn't mean to hurt you, but I thought maybe you felt the same way. I thought –"

Sharon interrupted. "I'm out of here. You've wasted enough of my time." And with that she stomped out of the shop.

Brad was astounded. That wasn't how he had expected things to go at all. He didn't want to be alone, so he decided to swing by Ben and Lisa's to talk things through.

When Olivia got home from her visit with Nonna, Nora welcomed her by having the apartment clean and a chicken roasting in the oven. When she opened the oven to stir the vegetables, the savory scent drew Olivia to the kitchen. They visited while the chicken finished cooking, and Olivia told Nora all about her week in New Orleans. A few days later her trunk arrived, and Olivia felt like it was her birthday. She unloaded the beautiful dishes, vintage tablecloths, vases, pictures and various odds and ends. They had a great time setting it all up.

When they were done, Nora admired her work. "You know, Olivia, you're a natural at decorating. You should think about doing it for a living. Maybe Maple View would offer a class you could take. At least you could try and see if it's something you'd really be interested in doing."

"Do you think I'm cut out for that?" Olivia loved to decorate but was doubtful she could make a career of it.

"Look at what you've done to this apartment! It's like a picture straight out of a magazine!"

The next night, Olivia and Nora borrowed Eric's car to make the twenty-five minute drive to Maple View Community College. She was excited to check out the interior design program. Olivia surprised herself and decided to sign up for a class. At the least, she'd have fun and maybe, *maybe*, she'd find her niche.

Monday morning Jake was waiting at the office door for her. He held onto her and kissed her until she was breathless. She pulled back a little to gaze into his eyes. "I've missed you so much, Jake." He kissed her again until they heard a cough.

Eric was walking up the sidewalk. "Save it for later!" He tried to make it seem like a joke, but Olivia could tell he was uncomfortable. She turned pink and unlocked the door. After more than a week apart, she had been so happy to see Jake that she forgot about where they were!

All day at work, every time she looked up, Jake was gazing at her. It was hard to focus on her dictation notes, and she yearned for time alone with Jake so they could catch up. That evening, they decided to go out for dinner instead of waiting until their usual Friday date.

Once seated in a cozy booth at the back of the restaurant, Jake held her hand as Olivia told him about her trip and design class. "I feel terrible. I've talked about myself this whole time. How was your trip, Jake?"

Jake's face darkened for a moment. "It was hard. My family and I fought. I don't want to talk about it."

After an awkward pause, Olivia changed the subject and soon they were on safe ground again. They chatted a while longer and then headed home. At Olivia's door, Jake held her tight. "Let's not ever be apart for that long again. It was too hard." Olivia lay her head on his shoulder and promised. *I wish he'd trust me with his heart like I trust him with mine.*

Several weeks had passed since Brad talked with Sharon, and she had not come to church or Bible Study during that time. Lisa tried to call a few times, but Sharon refused to talk to her. Her response confirmed to Brad that he had made a wise decision. She was not who he'd thought she was, but he also realized he was ready to find someone. It had been nice to have someone to go on dates with. He *did* want a family, and he was done with college and settled in his position at the school and in Glenn Haven.

At the next Bible study, he stayed late to talk with Ben and Lisa. After the last person had straggled out, they sat around the table. "I have a favor to ask you guys." They leaned forward, ready to do whatever they could for him. "Will you pray that God will bring the woman into my life I'm supposed to marry?"

Lisa let out an exasperated sigh. "I thought you were going to tell us you were dying or something! Of course we'll pray for you to find Ms. Right!" Ben and Brad laughed at her enthusiasm.

"You have to let *God* bring her, Lisa," Ben warned. "Don't go playing matchmaker." He reached for her hand and kissed it in affection.

Brad watched them and hoped that God would give him someone that would bring him as much joy as Lisa brought to Ben.

Chapter 7

Things at class were going well. Olivia's professor proclaimed she was a natural and encouraged her to pursue a career in interior design. Olivia returned home that night and asked Nora what she thought. "Do it, Olivia. You're so talented! You would be amazing!"

"Maybe I will." Olivia drifted to sleep that night amidst dreams of her future.

Friday night, she and Jake talked about what she should do. "That would be a great career for you, Olivia! Just think. One day when we have a family, you could work from home." While he spoke, he gazed into her eyes. "I'm going to marry you, Olivia, you wait." Olivia's heart melted with those words. When he kissed her, she never wanted it to end.

As Christmas drew near, Jake talked more about marriage, but he still hadn't proposed. Olivia wondered if he was going to ask her on Christmas day. When she mentioned her hopes to Nonna, she was troubled that Nonna continued to caution her. "Olivia, you haven't even introduced him to our family and you haven't met his. I'm not saying he's not the one, but he's moving pretty fast. What's the hurry?"

"You'll love him, Nonna. He's not traveling home for Christmas, so you'll get to meet him. Please give him a chance because you know Mama won't."

"Of course I'll give him a chance, *Tesoro*. I just want you to be careful. Marriage is a huge step, and I want you to make the right choice."

"I know Nonna. I love you so much. Thanks for always listening and loving me. I wish I could talk to Mama like I talk to you. She still seems hurt that I moved out. When will she see me as an adult?" Nonna encouraged her not to give up. Then they exchanged good-byes.

The week before Christmas, Olivia was closing up late. It was just her and Zig in the office. Jake left for a sales call, but they had plans to meet for a late dinner. Zig walked out to her desk. "Olivia, could you come into my office please?"

"Of course Zig, I'll be right in." Olivia walked in, and Zig closed the door.

"Sit down, Olivia. Something has come to my attention that I need to share with you."

Olivia's mind raced, what could it be? Did she make a big mistake at work? Was he letting her go? Zig grimaced and sat on the end of his desk. He cleared his throat. "I guess the best way is to come out and say it. I'm so sorry, Olivia, but I found out Jake is married."

Wide eyed, Oliva sat back in her chair. She couldn't believe it and was speechless. Zig had the wisdom to let the silence go for as long as Olivia needed. In her mind, she reasoned it all out. *He couldn't be. I know Jake, and he would never deceive me that way.*

"No, that can't be true. Zig, you must be mistaken."

Zig sighed and shared how he had found out. "When I was at that sales conference in Iowa, I ran into his old boss. He asked how things were working out with Jake and how he was handling the separation from his wife. I questioned him, thinking at first that he had confused him with someone else. But the more he talked, I knew we were talking about the same man. When I got back in town, I told Jake one of us was going to tell you. I think he thought I was bluffing. I gave him a few weeks, but it's evident that you still haven't been told. I'm so sorry Olivia."

Olivia stood up. "I have to go home." Zig held his hand out and told her again how sorry he was. Numb from the nightmarish news, Olivia gathered her things and walked out the door.

Olivia opened the apartment door and hung her jacket and purse on the coat rack. She wanted to be alone. Nora was in the kitchen preparing supper, and Olivia knew she had to talk to her whether she was ready or not. She walked into the kitchen and Nora turned around. Her eyes spoke volumes. She already knew. "Zig called me to make sure someone was here. I'm so, so sorry." Nora put on the water for tea and reached for Olivia's hand.

"I don't understand. How could I have not known? Oh, Nora, I held his hand, I kissed him, I told him I loved him and he said he loved me." As she wept, Nora rubbed her back and tried to comfort her. Nothing helped. Her heart was broken. The phone rang, and Olivia told Nora she didn't want to talk to anyone. From the rise in Nora's voice, Olivia knew who it was. She withdrew to her room. Nora could handle Jake.

Lisa woke up with a start, and she felt a strong urge to pray. She didn't know why, but she knelt by her bed and poured her heart out to God. She had never woken from sleep to pray. She didn't know who it was for, but someone somewhere needed it. All she could do was obey.

The next morning Olivia called Zig to tell him she couldn't make it in. Nora kissed her forehead before leaving for work at the bank.

"It's going to be okay Olivia. I'm here for you. You're going to make it through this." Olivia crawled back in bed, but couldn't sleep. The phone rang and Olivia reached over to unplug it. She wandered to the living room and stared out the window. The scene seemed to reflect her life. The sharp wind blew what was left of the leaves into the churning river, which swept them away like her dreams of a future with Jake. An hour passed in quiet despair, while tears ran down her cheeks like the raindrops on the window.

Then she saw him standing at the corner. He appeared miserable, cold and wet. He saw her at the window and walked to the door. She knew he was determined to talk to her. Olivia didn't know what to do. She loved him so much and wanted to hear him say it wasn't true, but knew in her heart it was. She battled with

Finding Hope

herself, but in the end decided to open the door so they could finish things once and for all. She pulled her robe closed. She was still in pajamas and looked awful, but didn't care.

As the door opened, in desperation Jake explained: "Olivia, please, I'm so sorry. I wanted to tell you about Susan, but I didn't know how." He began to cry. "I know I'm married, but not for long. It's over. Susan and I are separated. Please, please understand. I want to be with you!"

Olivia didn't know what to think. If he was separated and was going to file for divorce, maybe it was okay. She had a twinge of conscience, but then he pulled her into his arms and whispered words of love over and over. She knew his love for her was genuine. He leaned down and kissed her. At first she was still, afraid to open her heart to him. As the kiss grew in intensity, she quit thinking and clung to him. When they sank down into the couch, all thoughts of what was right were swept away like leaves in the river.

Olivia felt so confused and ashamed at what she had allowed to happen. "Olivia, it's okay. We're adults and we love each other."

"I know, but you're *still* married, Jake. Does your wife know about me? If it's over with her, have you told her you're seeing someone?"

"She already knows, Olivia. As soon as the divorce is final, I want to marry you." They decided to say good-bye for the afternoon. Olivia needed time to think.

When Nora got home they talked it out. "Come on, Olivia. If they're separated and he's filing for divorce, it's over anyway. He loves you and wants to marry you. We're not in the 1950's anymore. People get divorced all the time."

Olivia felt guilty, but she didn't want to lose Jake. She agreed to see him over the weekend. They met for dinner at a little cafe out of town and found a quiet table off to themselves.

"I'm sorry I didn't tell you sooner." As he held her hand and gazed into her eyes, he slipped a ring on her finger. Olivia gasped. "Olivia, I love you. I want to marry you. I want you to know how serious I am." Olivia was confused. He leaned over and whispered, "Come home with me."

The next morning the guilt was worse. He had a wife and a child. Could she do this? She left while he was asleep and took a walk by the river. She knew the right thing was to wait until the divorce was final. She wasn't super religious or anything, but she knew what she was doing was wrong. She didn't want to be the "other woman".

When he called later that night, she explained how she felt. "You're still married Jake. This isn't right."

"I know, Olivia, but when I'm around you I lose control. I love you so much." Jake tried to convince her there was nothing wrong with showing their love for each other, but agreed to slow down. Olivia sighed with relief. It was going to be fine. They had to be patient.

At work things were awkward. She could tell Zig and Eric were disgusted with Jake. She tried to explain, but they were too angry to hear what she had to say. She and Jake escaped the office at lunchtime so they could talk. Jake told her how frustrated he was that they were upset with him, and Olivia listened in sympathy.

The weeks dragged on, and Olivia grew tired of all the tension. It wore her out dealing with the guys at work. They were one angry word away from a knock-down, drag-out brawl. She needed to tell Eric to relax. While Jake was meeting with a client, she slipped into Eric's office to talk. They'd been friends forever, and she hated the distance this had put between them. He looked at her like he no longer knew what to say. "Oh, Eric, he does love me. His marriage is a disaster. He can't take it anymore. She sounds awful."

Eric sighed. "Olivia, how do you know that's true? He's a liar and a cheat." Olivia felt sick to her stomach, and she didn't want to lose one of her dearest friends over this. She decided to go home earlier than usual. Things were so hard, but it was worth it, wasn't it? At home she fell asleep in her bed before supper. Nora covered her up and turned out the lights.

When Olivia woke up in the morning, she was glad it was the weekend. She couldn't shake her fatigue. The whole situation was

Finding Hope

exhausting. How had things gotten so crazy? If her Mama found out – no, better not go there. If Mama found out all hell would break loose.

Olivia decided to go ahead and invite Jake to their family Christmas gathering. Mama, Papa and Nonna didn't need to know he was married. Soon the divorce would be final. At some point they'd meet his son, but even then they didn't have to know Olivia had dated him while he was still married.

On Christmas Day, Jake didn't seem to be nervous at all. He joked with Papa and was his usual charming self. Mama was cheerful which normally would've delighted Olivia, but she was terrified that somehow she would find out their secret. Nonna was quieter than usual. Olivia suspected she was less than impressed with Jake. The whole day was ruined. The attempt to act as if all was well had exhausted her. Christmas was the happiest time for their family, and she had been robbed of even that.

Olivia breathed a sigh of relief when Nonna left for New Orleans, and no one was the wiser about her situation with Jake.

New Year's Eve was always celebrated with gusto at the Grant's house. Ben and Lisa invited the usual group from Bible Study as well as most of Lisa's family. Ben's parents lived in Mississippi, so they weren't able to make it up for the party. Brad journeyed home to visit his parents in Kentucky over Christmas break, but this year Lisa talked him into to coming back a few days ahead of schedule for their party.

When Brad walked in around 11:30, he had to laugh. Lisa had hung streamers in all the doorways and was handing out Mardi Gras type masks at the door. The dining room table was loaded with all kinds of food, and each room was filled to capacity with people. Somehow even though space was limited, it didn't feel crowded. People were laughing and talking all over the house. Brad migrated over to where Ben and a few other friends were talking.

"Hey guys, sorry I'm late. Traffic was crazy around Indianapolis."

"No problem. We plunged ahead and started without you!" Ben gave him a grin. As the clock neared midnight, couples found each other and began the countdown. 10 - 9 - 8 - 7 - 6 - 5- 4 - 3 - 2- 1, Happy New Year!!! Brad was surrounded by couples kissing in the New Year. He slapped Ben on the back and maneuvered his way out of the room to find a plate of food.

Lisa joined him in the dining room a few minutes later to fix another plate for Ben. "Hey Brad, how was your time at home?" She balanced a plate in one hand and a cup in the other.

"Good. It was great to see my parents. My mom asked again if I had anyone special in my life." It had been an area of his life his mom tended to worry about. She was disappointed she didn't have any grandchildren yet. His brother, Brandon, had gotten married over the summer, and she was anxious to get the rest of her boys married off. "I wish I had someone to tell her about, but I can't force it."

"You're going to find someone amazing, Brad. Ben and I pray often that she'll show up soon. I had hoped it would be Sharon, but I think it's a good thing that didn't work out."

"I *know* it was a good thing. I haven't thought much about marriage or any of that until the last few months. Now that I'm ready, I'm much more aware of how alone I am." Brad knew he was being a downer and didn't want to ruin Lisa's night. "You'd better go get that food to Ben or he might starve."

"It's going to happen, Brad. I know it!" She headed back to the living room with Ben's food.

Brad slipped out and returned to his place earlier than he'd planned. He wasn't in a party mood.

Chapter 8

January 1979

When Jake walked into the office on Monday, he was dejected. He sat next to Olivia's desk and slumped over in the chair. "I don't know what to do, Olivia. I don't think I can wait much longer to be with you." She rubbed his arm and told him they'd make it. He glanced up, "I wish I'd have met you six years ago."

Olivia tried to lighten the mood. "Well, I would've been thirteen, so that might not have worked so well." He kissed her cheek as Eric walked in. Eric turned away and walked to his office and slammed the door. Olivia let out a sigh, and Jake returned to his desk.

That afternoon, Olivia and Nora were supposed to meet for lunch, and Olivia was running late. As she ducked into the restaurant, the scent of the tuna salad that Nora had ordered made her gag. She ran to the bathroom and threw up. *Ugh. Now what?* She hoped she didn't have the flu. Back at the table, she ordered a Sprite, and they talked while Nora ate. Madge pestered her to try and eat something, but she was afraid she might get sick again. Olivia dreaded going back to the office for another uncomfortable afternoon of silence.

The next day at work things were a little better. Eric stopped at her desk for a few minutes, the first he'd talked to Olivia or Jake since he found out. Zig came out of his office a few times. He had spent most of his time locked away with the door shut. Maybe everything was going to be okay. At lunch, Olivia and Jake chose Pauley's Pub. When he opened the door, the greasy smell of the burgers sent her reeling. She threw up in the bushes right outside the restaurant. "Are you okay, Olivia?" Jake stood behind her unsure of what he could do to help.

"I think I have the flu, Jake. Can you take me home?" When they pulled up to the apartment, he offered to come in and take care of her, but she wanted to be alone. When he left, she grabbed her calendar. She was terrified of what she'd find. She flipped back and figured how long it had been since her and Jake had been intimate. It had been 6 weeks, and she hadn't had a period since. She sank to the floor. It couldn't be. Jake wasn't divorced yet, and she had begun design school a few months ago. She sat in silence. When Nora walked in the door and saw her sitting on the floor, she ran to her.

"Olivia, what's wrong? What happened?"

Olivia looked up at her, resigned to the turn her life was about to take. "I'm late, Nora."

Nora gasped and sat down next to her. "Are you sure?"

"I'm sure."

"It could be anything. It's been so stressful for you the past few weeks."

"No, I've been sick, my skirts are tight, and I'm exhausted. What am I going to do if I'm pregnant?"

Nora tried to reassure her. "We'll make you a doctor's appointment. It's going to be fine, you'll see."

Dr. Batten's office was able to squeeze Olivia in the following afternoon at lunch. Nora agreed to go with her for the test. They sat in silent tension while they waited on the results. Twenty minutes later a nurse came in. "It was positive. You're pregnant!" she announced in a congratulatory tone, oblivious to the tension that filled the room. "We can't do anything until you're further along though. So we'll make an appointment for about a month out." She gave Olivia some paperwork and left the room.

"Oh no, oh no, oh no. What am I going to do?" Olivia began to panic. "He's still married, and I know Mama will disown me. What am I going to do?" For the first time in her life, Nora was speechless

Later that night Olivia called Jake. "I'm coming over, and we need to talk."

"Of course, Olivia, whatever you need." When she got there, he took one glance at her puffy eyes and pulled her on his lap on the couch. "It's okay. You can tell me anything, and you don't ever have to worry."

She laid her head on his shoulder and blurted it out. "Jake, I'm pregnant." He was silent. Olivia waited for him to process the news.

He gently moved her aside and stood up. Nothing was said as she allowed the news to sink in. He paced back and forth for several minutes, then sank back onto the couch next to her and put his head in his hands. "Are you sure? Maybe you're late?"

"No, the doctor confirmed it."

He looked worried but pulled her close; the only comfort he had to offer. "We're going to get married and be a family!" He reassured her it was going to work out.

Olivia gulped. She had decided to lay it all out there at once. "Jake, there's something else. I need to tell my parents." He wrapped his arms around her and told her he'd be there beside her. He'd always be there.

Olivia called Mama and set up a night to have dinner together. When they arrived her parents greeted Jake and made some uncomfortable small talk. They seemed to know something was wrong. Olivia knew she had to get it over with. "Mama, Papa, we need to talk." She'd never seen Jake so nervous. They all sat down.

"What is it?" Mama was never one to beat around the bush.

Olivia took a deep breath. "I'm pregnant."

Mama's expression was horrified, and Papa was dumbfounded. "Well," Mama spoke in a voice that seemed to be filled with venom. "I can't say I'm surprised. I knew something like this would happen."

"It was a mistake, Mama. We never meant for it to happen." Olivia's words fell on deaf ears.

"You'll have to be married right away, and we're not paying for a big wedding. I'm so ashamed. I can't believe you would dishonor your father and I this way." Olivia turned toward her dad, but he wouldn't make eye contact. "We'll go to the justice of the peace this weekend and that's that." Mama turned towards Jake.

"Do you have a place to live for my daughter or will you be living in someone's basement?"

Jake cleared his throat. "I'm so sorry ma'am. I never meant for this to happen." Olivia's mother ignored him.

"Mama, we can't get married yet." Olivia trembled. She knew that the coming news would destroy her mother.

"Oh yes you can, and you will!"

Olivia gathered her nerve. "Mama, he's married." Her mom was speechless. Olivia dropped to her knees, "Mama, please, please forgive me. I'm so sorry. I didn't know he was married at first. By the time I found out, it was too late. I was in love. He loves me, and he's getting divorced. We plan to get married. I'm so, so sorry!"

Olivia's mother turned, walked to her room and slammed the door. Olivia still knelt on the floor, her shoulders shook as she sobbed. Jake stood there with her dad in silence. Olivia peered up. "Papa?" A tear ran down his cheek, and Olivia's heart broke.

Neither she nor Papa could get Mama out of her room. Olivia and Jake left after several attempts to apologize, spent from the emotion. They drove to the beach and watched the waves come in. Olivia cried while Jake held her.

The next day at work, Jake's car wasn't there when Olivia arrived. She was concerned because he was often there at the same time as her, if not before. She walked in and Eric was waiting for her. The mood was somber. "Olivia, can you come in my office for a few minutes?" He held the door open for her.

Oh no, thought Olivia, *what now? I can't handle anything else.* She sat in the chair and he handed her a note in Jake's handwriting:

Olivia, I love you so much, and I have to do what's best for you. After last night, I realized this will never work. If we were to get married, I wouldn't be able to support you and the baby, plus Susan and my son. It's not fair to you. I know you don't understand, but in the end you'll be better off without me. Susan agreed to work things out if I promise never to see you again. Her

dad offered us a house in Iowa so that I can move away from here and start over. I'm going to work at his factory. I leave this weekend. I will always love you.
    Jake

    Olivia sat in stunned silence as time, it seemed, stood still. She noticed Eric couldn't meet her eyes. He peered at the floor and offered, "I'm so sorry Olivia. I don't know what to say. Jake came in this morning and told me he decided to go back to his wife. He asked me to give you this note." She stood up and walked to her desk. There was nothing to do but work. She had a baby to support and care for.

    Pregnant. Alone. Unwed mother. The words that ran through Olivia's mind frightened her. The break up with Jake had been so sudden; it hadn't quite sunk in yet. She knew she had someone else to think of now though. So despite her desire to protect her privacy, she set up her first doctor's appointment. Nora offered to go with her, but Olivia knew it was time to grow up and face her responsibilities.
    By the time of her appointment, Olivia was a bundle of nerves. She forced herself to walk into Dr. Batten's office. She resigned herself to the fact that she would soon receive judgment even from strangers.
    The nurse led her to the scales: one hundred and eight pounds. At least the nausea was going to help her stay trim. Not that it mattered because there was no one around to notice. Her blood pressure was taken and her urine tested. Left alone with her thoughts, she waited to meet the doctor.
    Dr. Batten barged in the room and Olivia jumped. This doctor was not at all what she had expected. She was short, round and had an impish smile. Olivia couldn't help but smile back. "Hello, I'm Dr. Batten, but please call me Dr. B. I do things differently than most doctors. I will be the one to see you at appointments and, barring any unforeseen circumstance, I will also deliver your baby."

Dr. B plopped her ample behind on the stool, and it protested as she rolled over to the exam table. She put her hand on Olivia's. "Now, I saw in your chart that you're unmarried, and you have chosen not to list the father's name." Olivia started to speak up, but Dr. B held up her hand. "I have done this long enough to see all kinds of situations. I'm here to be your doctor, not your judge. Any information you give us is confidential and used to provide you with better care. I know this is scary to face alone, and we're here to help you make the transition into motherhood as smooth as possible."

Olivia didn't know what to say. She was overwhelmed. After the exam, Dr. B gave her a due date of September 23rd. She left the office with a prescription for vitamins and nausea, some pamphlets on pregnancy, and another appointment scheduled. Olivia felt relieved after meeting Dr. B. It was a comfort to know that she would be treated with dignity and kindness.

Things at work were awkward to say the least, and Olivia hadn't even told Zig and Eric she was pregnant. She decided she'd let them figure things out for themselves. Eric still hadn't warmed up to her. She knew that their friendship had changed forever.

Things were even changing at home with Nora. Olivia was always so tired after work, and Nora wanted to have fun. They hadn't fought or anything like that, but Olivia could feel the distance that had grown between them. Their lives were headed in different directions, but Nora didn't seem to notice. She was always out on dates and had an active social life, and Olivia began to withdraw.

The weeks seemed to drag on, and Olivia felt loneliness settle in. She didn't know where to turn, but she *did* know she couldn't go home. Mama still wouldn't even speak to her. She hung up every time Olivia called. Papa didn't want to upset Mama, so he wasn't available to talk either.

One day she was sitting on her bench by the river, and a woman walked up and sat down next to her. Olivia scooted closer to the end, with hopes that the woman would leave her alone. No such luck.

"Hi, I'm Hope. You look so familiar, have you been to my art studio downtown?"

Olivia nodded, "I have. I bought some pictures of yours for my apartment a few months ago." Olivia gazed back out at the river, not really in the mood for chitchat.

After a few minutes of silence, Hope turned towards her. "I know this is weird, but I feel like I'm supposed to invite you to Bible Study at my friend's house."

Olivia laughed. *It's a little bit late for that.* Hope seemed to see the battle going on in her head. "Why don't you come with me and check it out? If you decide it's not for you, I won't pressure you to come back."

Olivia turned back to the peaceful, flowing river. "I'm uncomfortable going to church, Hope. If you knew what I've done, you would understand."

"Olivia, we all make mistakes. That's why we need God in the first place! Don't worry though. This Bible study is held in someone's home. Most of the group is around your age, and they are laid back and will welcome you with open arms."

Olivia continued to look straight ahead, wishing the river could take her away to – anywhere.

Hope lovingly continued. "Not all of them are church goers, so I think you'll feel pretty comfortable there. We have some great discussions about life, and we also laugh a lot." Olivia was reluctant, but agreed to try it. After all, what could it hurt? She knew she needed something different, so maybe it was worth a try.

In the morning, Olivia told Nora about running into Hope at the park and her decision to attend Bible study. Nora wasn't interested. "I love you, Olivia. You're fine the way you are. Things are hard enough right now, and going to a Bible Study won't change that." Olivia finished her breakfast and got ready for work. There wasn't much more to say.

Tuesday night, Olivia waited outside her apartment for Hope. She needed a few minutes away from Nora's skepticism. As she climbed into the car, her nerves got the best of her. "Maybe this isn't such a great idea, Hope. Could the two of us meet alone for now?"

"Olivia, don't worry. You'll be welcome there. It's a great group, and you're going to fit right in."

Olivia sighed and leaned back in her seat. "Okay, let's go."

As they walked into the little house, Olivia was surprised. Instead of sitting around a table with Bibles and notebooks, pens poised ready to take down every word, the group was gathered in the living room. Several people sat on the mismatched furniture and a few old crates, but most people were seated on the floor.

The host couple, Ben and Lisa, made her feel right at home. She found a place next to Hope on the rust-colored shag carpet, and several of the ladies introduced themselves.

When Brad saw Olivia walk through the door, he was mesmerized. He leaned over toward Lisa. "Who is that?" he whispered. He was unprepared for how strong his reaction was to this woman.

"She's the girl Hope met at the park last week. She's never been to church, so Hope invited her to Bible study. I guess she's shy."

Brad studied her while she found a seat and chatted with the women around her. She was beautiful, with her waist length black hair and petite build. Her eyes seemed to hold a depth he had wanted to see in Sharon, but wasn't there. Brad sensed there was something about her. He leaned back over to Lisa. "That's the woman I'm going to marry."

Lisa gave him a questioning glance because Brad wasn't one to say something like that. "You'd better get the lesson started and do introductions. That way you can find out her name before you propose." She tried to catch Ben's eye, but he was deep in conversation with Chuck and Drew.

Brad laughed. That was obvious, but he had never been so sure about anything in his life. This was the woman God had for him and an answer to his prayers.

As the group quieted down, Brad started talking. Olivia assumed he was the pastor. He gave a lesson on practical ways to serve God, and Olivia found herself fascinated with the idea that she could ever do anything for God.

As they closed, Brad asked for prayer requests and several people shared. Olivia hadn't expected them to be so honest and open. She glanced around to see if anyone was appalled when Gina shared she was struggling to quit smoking, but no one seemed to be bothered. They shared different struggles and then prayed. She had planned to go just once to appease Hope. She was sure she wouldn't fit in, but instead found herself drawn to these people.

On the way home, she told Hope she thought her friends were wonderful. She shared how surprised she was that the pastor was so young. Hope laughed.

"Oh he's not the pastor. He's our Bible study leader – and a neat guy. All the single girls are crazy about him!" Olivia could imagine. He was tall and trim with dark hair that curled at the ends. He had a warm smile and was a great teacher. She guessed there weren't many good-looking single guys at church.

Olivia grew quite pensive. *That's a problem I'll never have to worry about. No Christian man would ever want me now.* Hope sensed her change in mood and they spent the rest of the ride in quiet. When Hope pulled up to Olivia's apartment, she asked her if she would like to be picked up next week or not.

"I think I would like that, Hope. Thanks for inviting me. I had a nice time." Hope was filled with relief. She had such a burden for Olivia and prayed she'd feel comfortable with her friends at Bible Study.

Olivia heard Nora banging around the kitchen when she walked in the door. She hurried in and sat at the table, excited to tell Nora about her evening. Nora wanted no part of it though. She was sure Olivia felt guilty and wanted to make up for her mistakes.

"I mean, come on, Olivia. Church is for people who want to seem like they have it all together."

"They're not like that, though. You should come one time and meet them."

"No way!" Nora slammed the cupboard doors shut. "I'm not interested – and *don't* ask me again."

Olivia left Nora in the kitchen and stormed to her room. Things around the apartment were becoming as uncomfortable as they had been at home. Would she *ever* find a place where she could be at peace?

Friday after work, Olivia decided she wanted a Bible. She called Hope and asked her where she should get one. Hope told her about a little Christian bookstore off Main Street and offered to go along and help pick out a version that would be easy to understand. Olivia didn't know there were different versions to choose from, so she was happy for the help.

At the store, they searched for a translation for a new believer. Olivia decided on a Living Bible translation called *The Way*. When they took it to the counter, she was surprised that Hope offered to pay for the Bible.

The cashier must have sensed she wasn't used to receiving a gift. "You might as well let her pay. I've never seen anyone who was able to dissuade her." The cashier then gave Hope a wink. Olivia couldn't believe that someone who didn't even know her could be so kind. It made here want to read her Bible even more.

On the way home, Olivia decided to tell Hope about her pregnancy. She knew before much longer it would be evident anyhow. "Hope, I need to tell you something before I come back to Bible study again. Do you have a few minutes?"

"Let me find somewhere we can talk, Olivia. Would you mind if we sat by the river? I know it's cold, but it's such a beautiful place."

"That's perfect."

Finding Hope

Once seated at their favorite little wooden bench, Olivia proceeded to tell Hope about Jake and how they fell in love soon after they'd met. She then shared about being blindsided when she found out that Jake was married. By the time she came to the end of the story and revealed her unexpected pregnancy, Olivia was in tears. Hope held her hand and encouraged her to go on.

"I'm so ashamed of myself, Hope. I want to come back to Bible study, but I know I can't pretend that I have my life together."

Hope turned to face her. "Olivia, no one has a perfect life – or a perfect past. We all make mistakes, and even those who may *seem* to have it all together have things they're hiding."

"I know what you're saying, and I agree with you for the most part. But this is the worst thing I could've done. Even my own mother isn't speaking to me. How can I ask strangers, strangers who are religious, to accept me?"

Hope wanted to say the right thing. Olivia was so fragile. "My favorite verse in the Bible is: 'All have sinned and fall short of the glory of God'. It doesn't matter to Him what we've done: whether it's lie, kill, steal, or even do something some see as harmless, like gossip. It's all sin." Olivia's tears had stopped by now, and she felt some strange attraction to what Hope was sharing.

"The good news is the Bible also says: 'For the wages of sin is death, but the gift of God is eternal life in Christ Jesus our Lord.' That means we all deserve eternal punishment for our sins, but God sent his Son Jesus to die in our place. If we believe this is true (that Jesus was God's son, He died for us and was raised from the dead) and we confess with our mouth that He is Lord, we have eternal life. We're forgiven, and our sins are no longer held against us."

Olivia pondered what Hope said as she watched the snow fall. The bare gray tree branches were now covered with beautiful white snowflakes that danced like glitter in the late afternoon sun. *Could it be that simple? He would forgive her even after her huge mistakes?*

"It seems like I'm getting judgment and rejection everywhere I turn lately. If God will forgive and accept me, I want that. I want to start over, Hope. I want to be forgiven." Hope prayed with her, and the tears flowed again; this time tears of joy. Olivia felt peace flood her soul for the first time in her life.

After church on Sunday, Brad asked Hope if they could talk.

"Sure, no problem. Let me get my things together, and we can sit in our Sunday school room. No one is in there now."

Brad met her in the classroom a few minutes later. "I'll get right to the point. I want to ask Olivia out. How do you think she would feel about that? Would it scare her away from Bible study?"

"Sit down, Brad. Lisa told me you were interested, but I decided to wait and let you bring it up."

Brad sat down and gave her his full attention, unsure of what she had to say.

"You already know Olivia is a new Christian. What you don't know is the circumstances that led her to her faith. I wouldn't share this with you if I didn't trust you, but you are our Bible study leader, and this news will be obvious soon."

Brad began to feel nervous and sat back in his chair. He knew whatever Hope had to say must be a big deal. She was not one to blow things out of proportion. She was level-headed and kind. He had a lot of respect for this older woman who had taken their young group under her wing. Nothing could have prepared him for her next statement though.

"Olivia is pregnant." Hope observed him, hopeful he was the kind of man she thought he was.

"Pregnant?" he repeated, even though he had heard her clearly. Hope nodded. "Is she married?"

"No, she's not married – or dating. The father abandoned her after she told him about the baby. She may share more of her story with the group later, but I wanted to let you know a little of her situation before you make a decision. Please don't think I'm trying to discourage you from asking. I think she's very special."

"Thanks for telling me, Hope. I have a lot to consider." The news had blindsided him. He knew before he made a decision that he needed to pray.

Finding Hope

The time soon came for Olivia's four-month appointment. She was anxious to see Dr. B and find out how the baby was doing. After the nurse weighed her, she sat on the exam table and contemplated how much her life had changed in the last six months. Olivia's thoughts were interrupted when Dr. B made her entrance.

"Olivia Martinelli, how's my favorite patient?" Olivia grinned. She had a feeling everyone was Dr. B's favorite patient.

"Pretty good. I'm not so nauseous anymore. Well, that and my pants are pretty snug." Olivia was pleased with her ability to be light-hearted.

Dr. B had Olivia lay down and then showed her an instrument. "This is called a Doppler. We use it to hear the baby's heartbeat." Dr. B squirted her stomach with cold, clear gel and moved the Doppler over it, searching.

At first it sounded like static, but then it became more clear. She heard a whooshing sound and looked up at Doc. She had a big smile. "That's your baby, honey!" Olivia was overcome with delight. *My baby! It's real! I'm going to have a baby.*

The excitement surprised Olivia. She had spent so much time grieving over Jake and wondering how she was going to make it as a single mother, that she had never thought about the miracle taking place in her body. Add to that the miracle of her newfound faith, and it was almost too much to take in. Doc helped her sit up and told her that, over the next month or two, she would start to show and begin to feel the baby move.

Later that night, Olivia knew she had to call Nonna. She had been avoiding it ever since she found out she was pregnant. She wondered if Mama had already told her. It would be just like Nonna to give her time to adjust and bring the subject up herself. Her hands began to shake when she picked up the phone. She knew Nonna would love her no matter what, but hated the thought of disappointing her.

"Hello," the sound of Nonna's voice calmed her.

"Hi, Nonna, it's Olivia." She paused, unsure of how to go on. "I'm sorry I haven't called in a while."

"It's okay, *Tesoro*, your Mama called me. I knew you needed some time to let things sink in. You've been dealt quite a blow. It breaks my heart that you have to go through this. I wish I could be there with you."

Olivia began to cry. "I'm so sorry, Nonna. I know you warned me about Jake from the beginning. I let you down. I let my parents down. I'm so, so sorry."

Nonna listened to Olivia's regrets and told her over and over again she was loved. "Nothing you could ever do would cause me to be ashamed of you. It's going to be okay, Olivia. I'll be there for you every step of the way."

Olivia hung up with the promise to call again soon. She was up late that night as she thought of Jake. She tried to keep him out of her mind, but in her loneliest times she would wonder what her life *could* have turned out like if they were together. Many of her friends were feminists and would be appalled at her, but all she'd ever wanted was a family.

Olivia arrived late to work the next morning; something she had never done before. Zig didn't chastise her with words, but she she could see disapproval written all over his face. She sighed. *This office is no longer a happy place.* The camaraderie they had all shared before Jake came had been replaced by a tension she had no idea how to ease.

Zig and Eric had been kind and sympathetic when Olivia first found out Jake was married. But when she continued to date him, the sympathy had turned to disgust. She knew she deserved it, but longed for things to return to the way they were.

The one bright spot was Bible study and the friends she had made there. Each week she learned something new from Brad and was encouraged and loved by the others in attendance. Without this group, Olivia knew she would have been in despair. Since she had begun to attend, she found a reason to hope and felt a peace that had never been there before. It was strange how something so

Finding Hope

painful had caused a change that she hadn't even known was needed.
God, what else do you have in store for me?

Chapter 9

The more time Brad spent around Olivia, the more confident he became that she was the one. He had wrestled in prayer with God. He knew Olivia was young in her faith and vulnerable in her situation. It was a lot to think about before asking her for their first date. He didn't want to rush into something and see her end up hurt more than she already had been. He prayed for several weeks until he felt peace. Once he decided to ask Olivia out, he thought maybe it would be more comfortable to make it a foursome. Ben and Lisa would be sure to go along, and it would also help with the awkwardness that was sure to come along with their first date.

Wednesday night Olivia ventured out to buy a pair of maternity pants. She had been wearing her pants with a rubber band around the button to accommodate her growing waistline, but it wasn't working anymore. As she wandered around the maternity store and saw all the couples, she felt sad. She didn't miss Jake anymore. He had hurt her so much and proven himself to be a man who couldn't be counted on or trusted, but she didn't want to be alone either. She wondered what it would be like if things were different and he hadn't been married. A tear escaped and Olivia reached into her purse. Tears came often now and sometimes without warning. She learned to always keep tissues in her purse.

Olivia found a pair of pants to try. *They are so much more comfortable,* she thought, as she observed herself sideways in the mirror. As long as she wore a long shirt, her pregnancy was still hidden, but it wouldn't be much longer. She wondered how people would treat her once they knew. Would she still be welcome at Bible study? Would things change yet again at work? These questions often plagued her at night.

When Olivia got home that evening, Nora was gone again. She decided to call her mom, but as soon as Mama heard Olivia's voice she hung up. Olivia was devastated. She pulled out her Bible. The time she spent in quiet had been such a comfort. Hope had given her another verse to read and memorize: *Trust in him at all times, O people; pour out your heart before him; God is a refuge for us. – Psalm 62:8* The words she read seemed to envelope her in peace. She was in desperate need of a place of refuge, and she had found one. It was as if God were with her right in her room.

Olivia had always assumed the Bible was full of stern judgments, lists of things not to do, and cruel punishments. She was enthralled to read of all the mistakes God's people made and how He continued to forgive them. Of course, there were consequences, but God always seemed to love His people in spite of their sin. Most helpful was the practical instruction on how to live a different way. Olivia had been enlightened, forgiven, comforted, inspired, and given hope that life could be different for her and this little one.

Brad taught from Psalm 68 that week at Bible study. Two verses in particular caught her attention: *Father to the fatherless, defender of widows – this is God, whose dwelling is holy. God places the lonely in families; He sets the prisoners free and gives them joy ...* Olivia felt great comfort when she heard that verse. The thought that God would care for her and the baby she carried overwhelmed her.

Olivia decided to stay up later than usual, so that she could talk with Nora. Since the break-up with Jake and the fatigue from the pregnancy, Olivia chose to stay home most nights. Nora had an active social life and enjoyed her freedom, so that meant Olivia spent many nights alone. The distance that had grown between them saddened Olivia. She hoped they would get back to normal as time passed. When Nora arrived, she hadn't expected to find Olivia still awake.

"Are you okay?" she asked, concerned that something else had happened.

"Nothing's wrong, Nora. I wanted to talk with you for a few minutes. I have another appointment in a few weeks and wondered if you wanted to come with me. You could hear the baby's heartbeat."

Nora's eyes opened wide in surprise. "You can hear the heartbeat this soon? That's incredible!" She agreed to come along. Olivia was thrilled to have someone share with her this wonder of new life.

Olivia was pleasantly surprised at work the next day when Eric asked her to lunch. They hadn't done anything together in months. They talked over burgers about her new friends and the hope and peace she found through Jesus. Eric was happy that she was moving on from the "Jake fiasco" as he called it, but he was uninterested in her new faith. It was so hard that the friends she wanted most to share this with were not interested. Olivia decided it was best not to push it. She was thrilled to have Eric talk to her again.

The following week at Bible study, before she left, Brad approached her. "Olivia, would it be okay if I called you this week? I'd like to take you out for dinner sometime." Olivia was speechless. Completely caught off guard, she agreed to go.

As soon as they got in Hope's car, Olivia panicked. "Hope, did you know Brad planned to ask me out?"

"He mentioned it."

"I can't, Hope. He has such high standards, I could never live up to them. I imagine this worrying will be unnecessary once he finds out I'm pregnant anyhow. I agreed because I was caught off guard."

"I know he's intense, he'll soften though. He just needs a good woman, and he knows you're pregnant and asked anyway. Why don't you give him a chance?"

"He knows I'm pregnant?"

"Yes. He came to me for advice about asking you out, and I felt you would want him to know. I didn't give any details. I thought it would be easier on you if I told him. The fact that he still chose to ask you out means he's serious."

"I can't believe he's okay with it. It's all so unexpected, I don't know if I'm ready. It doesn't seem like the right time. My main focus right now is to know Jesus and adjust to the fact that I'm about to become a mother."

"I don't want to meddle, but you might want to think about it before you say no. Brad is a kind man, and he's not one to toy with your emotions. I'm sure he's prayed and moved forward with a lot of thought. You never know, Olivia. Maybe it's a God thing."

"I'll think about it – I promise." Hope offered to pray with her. Olivia bowed her head and once again felt the peace of God wash over her. When she lay down in bed later that night, she was able to sleep instead of spending the night in worry.

Nora met Olivia at Dr. B's the next morning before work. She was thankful for these early appointments. Otherwise she'd have to explain about her pregnancy, and she wasn't ready to do that yet. Doc squirted some more of the clear gel on her belly, and Nora's eyes widened as she saw Olivia's bare stomach.

"Oh my gosh, Olivia, I hadn't noticed with the clothes you wear. You're showing!" The sound of the baby's heartbeat filled the room, and an expression Olivia couldn't decipher came across Nora's face.

"Everything is right on track, Hun." Doc finished up the exam and helped Olivia sit back up. "Come back in four weeks."

When they got home Nora was quiet, which was unusual. Olivia didn't think much about it because she was lost in her own thoughts. That night at dinner she could tell something was wrong. "Okay, Nora, what's wrong?"

Nora sat down and hung her head in regret. "I can't do it."

"Can't do what?"

"I don't want to have a baby here. I am so sorry. I guess I haven't thought all of this through. I'm single, and I want to live the single life. I don't want to live with a baby. It's so much responsibility."

Olivia was overcome. This was a thought that had never crossed her mind. *Where will I go? How will I pay for an apartment on my own? How will I survive?* Her mind raced with yet another uncertain future. She was ostracized by her family. Jake's leaving had devastated her. Now Nora wanted to desert her. Money was a big issue. There was no way she could cover full rent and a babysitter on her modest income.

Nora avoided eye contact when she said, "You have a few more months before the baby comes, but you should start to search for a new place before too much longer."

Olivia didn't know what to say. She couldn't eat. She scraped her dinner in the trash and placed her plate in the sink. Then walked down the hallway to her room. She wasn't angry – or sad. She wasn't anything – except numb. She took her clothes off and hung them in the closet. She put on her pajamas, closed the curtains and slipped into bed. It was 6:30 p.m. on a beautiful spring evening, but all she could think about was sleep.

The next day at work, Olivia found several phone numbers to nearby apartment complexes. Unless she was about to get a promotion, which she doubted, there was no way she could pay the rent at any of them. She stood up to stretch, and at the same time Eric walked out his office. His eyes traveled down to her stomach, and his mouth dropped open.

"Oh, Olivia – oh no." He rushed to her and hugged her. She began to cry, but not for the reason he thought. She was relieved he knew.

As he gawked at her, a nervous laugh escaped her, "Surprise!"

Eric didn't laugh. "Why didn't you tell me, Olivia? I'll kill him."

"No, Eric, I'm okay. I'm going to be fine." He saw a quiet confidence in her eyes. "I could use some help shopping for an apartment though. I have to find a place before the baby comes."

Eric sighed. "Nora not up to the inconvenience of a baby?"

"I don't know why I ever thought it would work. Nora is a free spirit. She wouldn't want to step outside to smoke or turn her music down while the baby slept. It makes me sad because I loved living with Nora, and I'm kinda scared to be alone."

Right then, she felt it – a tiny kick. It was as if her baby was reminding her that, from now on, she wouldn't be alone. It would be the two of them.

Eric told Olivia that he had a friend who lived in an apartment complex, Vine Hill, that charged rent based on your income. They found the name in the phone book, and she decided to call and make an appointment for after work.

Eric tagged along with Olivia to look at a two-bedroom apartment. The waiting list was six months long, but she decided to put her name down anyway. She had 3 ½ months until the baby was due, but she was hopeful something would open up.

Olivia couldn't believe she had let Brad talk her into a date, and she was grateful Ben and Lisa would join them. They had decided to play miniature golf and go out for pizza afterwards. She searched in desperation for something to wear that didn't show her growing belly, but she was out of luck. It didn't seem right to go on a date with Brad while she carried Jake's baby.

Tears welled up in her eyes, and she thought about how her life had veered so far off the course she had planned. Jake was supposed to be with her, and they should be settling down to a life together. Maybe a shotgun wedding; but no wife on the side. Nora peeked in Olivia's room and saw that she was a nervous wreck. Instead of comforting words, she questioned the kindness of Olivia's new friends.

"If they're so great, why are you scared? It seems like, if they are so kind and loving, you'd be fine."

Olivia sighed, tired of being on the constant defense against Nora's accusations. "It's not like that, Nora. It doesn't seem right; me on a date while I'm expecting someone else's child. I don't want to ruin his reputation." Nora snorted in disgust and walked out.

Olivia decided to sit on the porch to wait. Spring had arrived, and she preferred the quiet beauty of the river over Nora's attitude. Once outside, Olivia was startled to see Miss Elva. She had been gone for the winter, and Olivia hadn't realized she was back.

"Welcome home, Miss Elva! Did you enjoy Florida?"

"I did! I spent my days at the beach and the senior center; much better than time here in the North Pole." She and Olivia laughed.

Miss Elva's keen eyes took in Olivia's pregnancy. "It seems I missed a lot over the winter. Did you and your young man get married?"

Eyes downcast, Olivia shook her head. Miss Elva reached over and took her chin in her hand. "You don't need to be ashamed in front of me, missy. My life is far from perfect. If you ever need to talk, you come down and we'll have some tea and sort things out."

Olivia hadn't anticipated the strength she received from Miss Elva. She had always taken her at face value: an eccentric old woman who kept life interesting. Now she saw something else; maybe Miss Elva had more to offer than she thought.

They sat together in comfortable silence until Brad, Ben and Lisa arrived. "I will be down to visit soon, Miss Elva. Thank you for your kindness."

"Get on with you, girl! Enjoy yourself – and relax!" Olivia grinned as Miss Elva shooed her away.

Brad walked Olivia to the car and opened the door. She slid in the back next to Lisa. Brad sat up front with Ben. They all visited and laughed at the stories Ben and Lisa told about their kids. Olivia was envious of the warmth Ben and Lisa had toward each other and the obvious love they had for their children. Lisa must have guessed she was feeling sad because, while Ben began another story about their son, James, she took the opportunity to lean over and squeeze Olivia's hand. She whispered that someday Olivia would have a family, too. Olivia was amazed how God used the new friends in her life to show His love for her.

She listened to Ben's story about their son; it sounded like he was something else. Ben told how Lisa had been doing laundry a few month back when she smelled smoke. First she ran up to the playroom where the kids were supposed to be, but Nicole was there by herself. She was sitting on the floor with her baby doll and pretending to feed it. She dashed back downstairs and found little James in the kitchen crouched down next to a pile of flaming tissue paper from a gift she had wrapped. When he heard Lisa enter, he looked up with a proud expression. "I built a campfire, Mommy. Now we can make s'mores!"

Olivia gasped, "Oh my word Lisa. What did you do?"

"Well, first I put the fire out. Then I told him how thankful I was that he wanted to do something special for me, but that fire was dangerous. We decided to color pictures together instead."

Olivia was startled. That's not how things would have played out had that happened when she was little.

When they got to the miniature golf course, Olivia visited with Brad. He was gentle and kind. He had a dry sense of humor that she hadn't noticed before. It helped set her at ease. After a round of miniature golf, they went out for pizza. Olivia noticed as they walked to the table that people gave them a smile when they saw she was pregnant. Brad didn't seem to mind, but all she could think about was how selfish she was to put him in this situation. To ask him to accept her pregnancy was too much. By the end of the night, Olivia was ready to go home. Everyone was so nice, but she felt awkward and conspicuous being with Brad.

Olivia was relieved when they pulled back up in front of her apartment. She thanked everyone and started to climb out of the car. "Wait a minute. Let me get your door." Brad jumped out before she had a chance to argue.

He opened the door and walked her to the front porch. "I had a lot of fun tonight, Olivia. I'm so glad you agreed to come along." She had planned to tell him this wasn't a good idea but couldn't do it. He was just so great. *Maybe it will get easier.*

"Thanks, Brad, I had fun as well. I'll see you next Tuesday." She watched him walk back to the car and waved as they drove away.

When Olivia walked in the front door, Miss Elva poked her head out. "I like this one, Olivia. I can tell he's a good one!" With that she closed the door, leaving Olivia alone in the entryway. She smiled to herself as she walked up to their apartment. *Oh, he's a good one alright.*

All week after work, Olivia and Eric spent time perusing the classifieds for apartments in her price range. She hadn't heard from Vine Hill, and her due date was fast approaching.

"Hey, Olivia, what about this one?" Eric asked. "It would be perfect, and it's still within walking distance of work so you still won't need a car."

They wrote the address down, but Olivia was hopeful the income based housing would work out. "I don't know how I'll make it without a roommate, Eric. I can't believe I'm doing this alone."

Eric set the newspaper down on the desk. "Olivia I'm so sorry. I wish I'd have known more about Jake before I set you guys up. I feel responsible, and now I don't know how to help. I wish I could make him be here for you. It's not right that he left you with no thought of what would happen to you and the baby."

"It's not your fault, Eric. He was so persistent; I would have ended up going out with him anyway. I wish things were different, too, but I *do* know I'm going to love this baby and provide a good home for us." Olivia wished Eric could understand how much it meant that he was there for her.

That night Olivia decided to approach Nora. The distance between them had to be addressed. She found her on the living room floor surrounded by bottles of nail polish. "Nora, we need to talk. I know our friendship will change when I move out and the baby is born, but you're my best friend, and I hate this wall that has come between us."

Nora explained how she felt frustrated with Olivia's new faith and new friends. All the changes were hard. "Don't get me wrong. I'm happy that you found something that makes you feel better about yourself, but I worry about these friends. I don't want you to get hurt by anyone else."

"But they're so supportive of me, Nora. I feel more loved and accepted than I ever have. It's not something that makes me feel good. It's changed my life." Olivia was hopeful that at last Nora would understand where she was coming from.

"Olivia, if you want things to be more open between us, you're going to have to accept that I don't trust them. You're not going to change my mind."

Olivia knew it was an area where they had to find common ground. "Your friendship means the world to me, and I don't want to lose it." They decided to call a truce and leave it alone from now on. Nora would quit the attitude when Olivia mentioned her new friends, and Olivia would quit asking her to come along and try to get to know them.

Olivia was glad they talked but felt sad. It was so hard to have all these changes and no one to share them with. Eric didn't get her faith either, but he wasn't antagonistic like Nora. Instead, he avoided the issue like the plague.

When Hope arrived to pick her up for Bible study on Tuesday, she noticed Olivia's discouragement. "What's wrong, my friend?"

"I feel so alone. My friends don't want to hear about what God is doing in my life. My parents still won't speak to me, and I have a baby to raise by myself soon. I'm overwhelmed." Hope pulled the car over, and Olivia turned toward her in surprise. "What are you doing? We'll be late."

"I want to pray with you. I can't imagine how scary all of this is. Do you mind?" Olivia bowed her head, and Hope held her hand. *"Dear Jesus, please be with Olivia. Give her Your perfect peace. I want to ask that You would do a miracle and open the door for restoration between her and her parents. I pray she draws near to You during this scary time. In Jesus' name, amen."*

Olivia was very moved by her prayer – and that she considered her more important than being on time. "Thank you, Hope. You have been such a wonderful friend to me."

They were about ten minutes late for Bible study, so they didn't have time to visit with anyone before they sat down. Brad caught Olivia's eye and smiled as he was giving the lesson. She was amazed that he had even considered dating her. After study was over, while they broke into groups of two or three and visited, Brad asked her if she'd come sit on the porch with him.

It was a warm night. The sky was clear, revealing the beauty of the stars. The full moon illuminated the trees. Brad had prayed about and debated the past several weeks whether or not to take the next step, and he decided it wouldn't hurt to ask. "Would you like to come to church with me on Sunday?"

"I don't know, Brad. I haven't been to church since I was a little girl. My parents attended on Christmas and Easter. This doesn't seem like the best time to show up." Olivia patted her hand on her stomach.

I know you're self-conscious about your pregnancy, Olivia. Some people will be judgmental. It happens at church like anywhere else. I think you'll find, though, that most will be like they are here at Bible study. They'll love and care for you."

Olivia agreed to go although she was nervous of how she'd be received. Brad offered to pick her up for church, so she didn't have to walk in by herself.

As they walked down the aisle at church, Olivia noticed the curious glances in her direction and could imagine what people were thinking. When they found their seats, Brad whispered that he'd be going up front to play guitar but that he'd join her for the sermon. While she watched him lead these people in worship, she knew. This wasn't right. Brad was an amazing man and he deserved an amazing woman; a woman without a tainted reputation and a child on the way. She made up her mind to break things off as soon as they had a chance to talk.

In the car she tried to explain to Brad. "I need to be alone right now. I have so much to deal with. I don't want to drag you into my mess – it's not fair. You deserve better than this."

"Olivia, I want to get to know you, but I respect your decision if you need some time right now. I can wait." Olivia knew it wasn't going to go any further. Once the baby came he'd lose interest. She

Finding Hope

was thankful that he was gracious though. "I will give you space, Olivia, but promise me you'll keep coming to church and Bible study. "I don't want you to feel uncomfortable around me because I'd be fine with you still coming to Bible study. Olivia climbed out of the car and waved good-bye to the kindest man she'd ever known.

Olivia decided to see if Miss Elva was up for some company, so she tapped on her door. "Come on in," she heard Miss Elva call out in a muffled voice. Olivia opened the door and saw Miss Elva on the floor trying to coax Giselle out from under the couch.

"She jumped on the counter and got a hold of a piece of chicken. I'm afraid she'll choke on the bone." Olivia watched as Miss Elva hauled her out and wrestled the bone from her mouth. "Blasted cat!" Mrs. Elva acted angry, but she adored her cat. Olivia tried not to laugh.

"Have a seat. Would you like some tea?"

"That sounds wonderful."

Once the tea was ready, Miss Elva took a seat across from Olivia. "How are you, girl?" Miss Elva knew how to get to the point.

"I'm okay. Sometimes I feel so alone. Nora and I don't spend time together like we used to."

"I know how that can be. Sometimes friends don't know how to respond when life takes an unexpected turn. We can't blame them, but it's tough." Miss Elva turned her gaze to the picture on her table. She picked up the frame and passed it to Olivia to examine.

"I was married to the most handsome man around when I was young. We had a beautiful little girl. Her name was Clara. We were happy – happier than most people are in a lifetime. One summer, when Clara was four and I was expecting our second baby, we decided to head to the beach.

Olivia was filled with dread. She knew this story wasn't going to end well. There were no pictures anywhere of another child and, after the age of four or so, there were no more pictures of Miss Elva's little family.

"It was a beautiful day, Olivia; the kind of day where it seemed nothing could go wrong. We were singing along to the radio and didn't even hear the train whistle. One minute I had the whole world and the next minute I had nothing. I lost all of them. My husband, my daughter, even the child I carried. They say it was a miracle that I survived. It sure didn't feel like one. For years, I wished I had died with them that day. It took me a long, long time to put the pieces of my life back together. My friends didn't know how to comfort me, and my family was so heartbroken that I often found myself comforting them.

"My situation seems so trivial compared to yours, Miss Elva. You lost everything."

"Pain is pain, girl. You can't compare losses. I tell you my story not to downplay yours but to show you that, in spite of your circumstances, you still have so much to look forward to! You have this sweet baby to love and, though you may not see it yet, someday you'll be glad things didn't work out with Jake. He is not the type of man you want to share your life with."

"You're right, Miss Elva. How did you recover from your loss? How did you find your zest for life again?"

"T-I-M-E. I thought I would die from the grief. But each day I woke up, I put one foot in front of the other until I made it to the next day. It took me *years* to even begin to feel like myself again. The same principle applies to you: time alone will lessen the pain. It may not ever be completely gone, and you will never be the same person you were before this happened, but you will get through this. You are going to be fine."

With that, Miss Elva ambled outside to work on her flower beds. Olivia knew the conversation was over but pondered her words the rest of the day.

Chapter 10

Monday was Olivia's six-month checkup with Dr. B, and she was excited to go. As she waited on the exam, she heard Doc making her way down the hall singing, "Yes sir, that's my baby / No sir, don't be maybe / Yes sir, that's my baby now." She was so thankful for her, and what a ray of sunshine she was. The door opened, and Doc called out her greeting, "Hello, Olivia dear! How are you feeling these days?" Olivia asked a few questions while Doc checked her out.

"Well, you've made it to the third trimester! Next appointment we'll set you up for Lamaze classes. Have you given any thought to who you'd like to have as a support person?" Olivia was sure Nora would be there. "Bring her along next time if you'd like, and we'll get you all set up."

The baby had become active, and Olivia loved to feel the kicks. At dinner, she asked Nora if she wanted to feel. While Nora's hand was on her stomach, Olivia decided to let her know about Lamaze classes. Nora looked at her in surprise. "You know I don't want to do that, Olivia. I have no desire to witness a birth. I couldn't be in there with my sister either – remember?"

"But this is different, Nora. Who else is there to even ask?"

Nora shook her head. "I'm so sorry, but I can't." They finished another dinner in silence. Olivia wondered how much more rejection she could take. A few hours later the phone rang, and Nora yelled that it was for her.

Olivia wondered who'd be calling this later. "Hello?"

"Hello, Olivia, it's Mama. Papa and I are going for supper this Friday, would you like to join us?"

Olivia was shocked because they hadn't spoken in months. "That would be fine." She waited, unsure of what else to say.

"We'll pick you up at 6:30." That was it, and then Mama hung up. Olivia knew she had experienced a miracle. Her mom reaching out in any way was huge. She stopped right then and thanked God for His kindness to her. That week at Bible study, Olivia shared about her upcoming dinner with her parents, and they agreed to pray for their time together.

Brad lay awake that night. He stared at his ceiling and wondered if he was crazy. How was it that he had fallen for a woman who had no interest in him and was pregnant with another man's child? He still felt she was the one God had for him but understood her need to be alone. Sleep was a long time coming as his mind wondered what God's plan was.

She has so much to face right now. If I can just be a friend, maybe once the baby is born I could try again. It's so hard to wait! The more I get to know Olivia, the more I want to help her – to make her life easier. I want to show her that all men aren't the same. After a short prayer, Brad finally dozed off.

That Friday night, Olivia headed out to wait on the porch at 6:20. Mama hated when you were late. She didn't want to cause any more trouble. Mama and Papa pulled in front of her apartment, and Olivia marveled again at how God had brought it all about. Even though dinner was uncomfortable as they skirted around the sensitive subject of her pregnancy, it was nice to be together. As flawed as their relationship was, she still wanted them in her life. Olivia shared with them about how she was hunting for an apartment and was on the waiting list at Vine Hill, but so far hadn't heard anything.

"What are you going to do if it doesn't open up soon?" Mama was never one to leave things to fate.

"If I don't hear anything by next weekend, I will start searching for an apartment to live in until one opens up at Vine Hill."

Papa had been even quieter than usual through the dinner. He let Olivia and Mama talk, and waited for his cue to say something. "Well, I guess I can drive and help you search then." Olivia was surprised that Papa had offered and even more so when Mama agreed it was a smart idea. They decided he'd pick her up next Saturday, and they would go hunt for an apartment together. As they stood to leave, Mama glanced down at her belly, and an expression of sadness flashed across her face.

"Let's get going, Papa. It's late." Olivia wished Mama would acknowledge the baby but knew they had made progress tonight. Upon arriving back at Olivia's apartment, Papa kissed her cheek. "We'll see you again soon." Mama used a stern voice to disguise her attempt to reach out, but Olivia knew she was trying. She waved good-bye from her front step and went inside feeling more lighthearted than she had in months.

Olivia's figure had changed over the last few weeks. She had gone from a tiny bump to an obvious pregnant belly that could no longer be hidden beneath a shirt. She was seven months along now and grew larger every day. She was anxious to find out if it was a boy or girl. Would it resemble her more or Jake? Would it bring pain to see a likeness of him? She was excited, but also getting more nervous as her due date drew near.

At the next Bible study, Olivia was out on the porch with Lisa and Hope. "How is your pregnancy going, Olivia?" Lisa asked. "You don't talk much about things, and I know you must have lots of questions. Is there anything you want to ask me?"

"I don't know what to even ask. I've never even *been* around a baby. I had no brothers or sisters, and and my cousins are all far away. Even though Mama and I have had a strained relationship since this happened, we would have never talked about it anyway."

"Olivia, you can talk to me anytime! I know how scary it is when you are pregnant the first time. Have you signed up for the Lamaze classes? They help a lot."

Olivia started to cry. "I don't have anyone to go with me for the class. I had hoped my roommate, Nora, would come, but she says she can't handle it. I am terrified of being alone in the delivery room."

Lisa gathered her into a hug. "Oh, Olivia, I would be honored to go to classes with you; and even the birth if you'll have me."

"You don't have to do that, Lisa. It's a huge commitment. I'm sorry I seem so needy. I don't want you to feel obligated."

"I *want* to. When do the classes begin?" Lisa had convinced Olivia that she was happy to go with her, and they made arrangements to attend the first class together. Olivia left that night with a load lifted from her shoulders.

Brad had watched the women take Olivia outside and saw her break down in tears. It tore his heart out to watch and have no way to help her. It was all he could do to stay inside and appear to be interested in anything other than what was taking place on Ben and Lisa's front porch. He knew that the one thing he *could* do for Olivia was pray, and he was already doing that.

Olivia and Lisa were on their way to the first Lamaze class, and she wondered if there would be anyone else there without a husband. The hospital was a few blocks away, so they decided to walk. It was mid-July, and Lisa suggested they stop by the Tasty Twist for a well-deserved ice cream cone after class. They arrived a few minutes before class started and chose a seat in the back. As the other couples trickled in, Olivia was dismayed that she was the sole woman without a spouse. Lisa squeezed her hand while they waited for class to begin.

Olivia was overwhelmed as they did an overview of the various subjects the instructor would be covering in class: IV meds, breathing methods, and delivery scenarios. She gave Lisa a helpless look. She had no idea what she had gotten herself into. Lisa leaned over and said, "Don't worry, I know all about this stuff. We'll talk about it after class while we eat ice cream." That sounded better than asking questions in front of a group of people she didn't know.

Olivia still hadn't heard from Vine Hill by Saturday, so Papa picked her up to go check out the apartment listings in her price range. The first was a house that was owned by an older couple who wanted to rent out the top floor they no longer used. It was at the end of a quiet street not too far from where Olivia had grown up.

A woman stood at the door to greet them. "Well, hello there. I'm Mrs. Easton!" She welcomed them in. She glanced at Olivia's stomach. "Oh, you didn't mention on the phone that you were expecting. How delightful. This house hasn't had a child in it in ages!" Olivia smiled. It was a huge relief to know the baby didn't concern Mrs. Easton. Papa still seemed uncomfortable though. "Well, would you like the grand tour?"

"Of course," Olivia agreed.

Mrs. Easton pointed out the updates she and her husband had done over the years. "Oh, you should have seen the nasty carpet that was up here before Mr. Easton replaced it. The window had leaked all winter and we didn't know." She wrinkled her nose in disgust. "We came up here last spring and it was full of mildew. I told Mr. Easton, 'You get that carpet out of here right now; otherwise it'll make us sick!' You wouldn't know it now, though. It's beautiful!"

She rambled on as she led Olivia and Papa through the quaint apartment. It was clean and the quality of the repairs was evident. Olivia knew she would feel safe here. She felt hopeful that this would work out, and even Papa appeared pleased.

When they returned to the kitchen, Mrs. Easton pulled a chair up to the table for Olivia and took a seat across from her. Papa remained standing nearby, still looking around. "What do you think?" She was eager to get things settled.

"I think it's just perfect! The baby and I won't need much space, and it's such a quiet neighborhood – " Olivia stopped. The woman's expression had changed.

"You and the baby? Aren't you married?" She asked in a scandalized voice.

Olivia's face turned red. "No, ma'am, I'm not," she stammered. The room was quiet for a moment, which seemed like an eternity for Olivia. Mrs. Easton glared at her like she was as worthless as the carpet they had removed earlier that year. She stood up in an abrupt manner.

"I'm not sure this will be the right fit for you after all. Thank you for stopping by." Mrs. Easton walked to the door, and it was evident they were being dismissed.

Olivia and Papa wasted no time returning to the car. Olivia was humiliated. Papa said nothing of the treatment they'd received. "Well, where's the next house?" When she gave him the address, he raised his eyebrows at her.

"Papa, I can't afford anywhere else. I'm out of options. Maybe it won't be that bad." They drove over in uncomfortable silence. When they pulled up to the house, the scene was depressing. It was a large, older home that seemed as dejected as Olivia felt. The paint had peeled. The concrete steps that led to the door were crumbling. Several women sat on the porch, their loud voices carried to the street and cigarette smoke swirled overhead. Children played in the front of the house. You couldn't call it a lawn because it was more dirt than grass. A few tufts grew near the sidewalk. Olivia took a deep breath and started to climb out of the car.

"No."

She turned, startled at Papa's firmness. "What, Papa?"

"No, you're not living here. I can't let you. We'll figure something out, but my daughter and grandchild are not living here."

Olivia sat back down. Papa *never* spoke up. "Okay, Papa, I'll keep searching – I promise." He dropped her off back at her apartment. Once inside, she disappeared into her room, lay across the bed and buried her head in the pillow. Where was she going to live? She didn't think she could bear the intense humiliation that she had experienced today. Olivia cried herself to sleep, brokenhearted.

At the following Bible study, Olivia decided to ask for prayer. She didn't go into much detail about all that had taken place because it was too painful. They all held hands and took turns praying that the perfect living situation would open up for her and

Finding Hope

the baby. That night after study, Hope and Lisa noticed Olivia was down and decided to take her out to cheer her up.

"Hey Olivia, Ben offered to watch the kids so I can go out for a bit. Do you want to join Hope and me for some ice cream?" Olivia was grateful to get out and laugh. Time with Lisa was guaranteed to be fun.

Ben pretended to grumble about getting the kids to bed by himself, but Lisa rolled her eyes and they all laughed. He kissed her on the cheek and told them to have fun – and not worry about anything.

Over hot fudge sundaes and mint chocolate chip ice cream, the girls ended up in a discussion about what labor would be like. Olivia and Hope laughed while Lisa entertained them with the stories of when James and Nicole had been born. "Each delivery is different. It's okay if you need some help with pain, so don't tell yourself that you are a failure if you ask for it. The goal is a safe delivery and a healthy baby, not a medal for some kind of toughness."

"Thank you so much, Lisa. It's nice to talk to someone who's done this before. I'm excited to meet this baby, but I have no idea what to expect."

"I felt that way both times. It's normal to be nervous." They talked a while longer, and then Lisa needed to leave. She wanted to make sure Ben had gotten James in bed. She sighed, "Last time I left for an evening when I got home the house was a disaster, the kids were awake and Ben was asleep on their bed. It's nice that they need me though." Olivia thanked her again and gave her a hug before they left. It was weird how people she'd known a few months were more like family to her than her own family had ever been.

A few days later Olivia got a call from Vine Hill. They had a vacancy; a two-bedroom unit that would be available in two weeks! That put her at two months before her due date. It was cutting it close, but it was such a comfort to know her baby would have a home.

When she sat down to tell Nora the good news, Nora began to cry. "I can't believe you're leaving. Things will never be the same."

Olivia teared up, too, but she couldn't help feeling a little excited. Her own apartment! Now she would have a peaceful, private place to learn how to be a mother; no one to watch her or judge her for the mistakes she was bound to make.

They hugged and then Nora jumped up. "Let's get you packed. You're getting so fat, you won't be able to bend over to pack the boxes!" she teased. They had a lot of fun over the next couple of weeks sorting through things. They laughed and talked like they hadn't in ages. Before she knew it, though, it was moving day. The guys from Bible study offered to help Eric and Papa move her belongings. Once they had unloaded the boxes and the few pieces of furniture Olivia had, Nora, Hope, Lisa and Gina helped her unpack and setup. They even brought her dinner.

After the moving crew left, Olivia was exhausted but happy. So many things had worked out that she had never expected. It was humbling to see how God took care of her even though she'd made so many mistakes.

Olivia called Nonna to let her know she was settled, but she was exhausted so they kept the call short. "I know you're tired *Tesoro*, but I want you to know how proud I am of you. Now, you go rest and we'll talk again soon." Olivia hung up and soon was in bed.

Chapter 11

It was August and time for another doctor's appointment. Doc helped Olivia lay back on the table and explained how appointments would change. "You are going to start coming in weekly now. I will check you and see if you have started to dilate. I'll also check for swelling and things like that."

Olivia held her breath while Doc performed the exam. "Is anything happening yet?" She was nervous to hear the answer.

"No, not yet. I expect you to go to your due date. First babies like to take their time."

Olivia felt relieved. *I'm not ready yet.* As September drew closer, she became more and more apprehensive.

At the next Bible study, Olivia felt weary. Lisa warned her the last weeks would be tough, but there was nothing to prepare her for how that felt. As they walked in she blinked her eyes in disbelief. Ben and Lisa's house had streamers and balloons everywhere. There was a cake and a huge pile of gifts.

She glanced around the room and saw her mom, Nora, Miss Elva, her friends from Bible study and a few ladies she didn't know. Hope whispered that they were from the church and had wanted to help. Olivia started to cry. She felt so unworthy to receive so much when she had done things so wrong. Hope and Lisa rushed to hug her, and Gina got their attention to start games.

After Olivia had opened the gifts, Lisa asked if anyone had any advice for the mama-to-be. Several of the older ladies from church went first. Mrs. Hall encouraged her to enjoy every moment because babies grow up fast. Mrs. Potter recommended she rest when the baby rests, and Mrs. Clark reminded her that every mother makes mistakes and not to be too hard on herself. Next was her Mama, and Olivia wasn't sure what she'd say.

"Keep up with the laundry." With that she nodded to the woman next to her, signaling that was all she had to say. Olivia had to smile. *That is typical Mama. Short and sweet. Well – not always sweet, but to the point.*

By the end of the evening, she had more things than she even realized she would *ever* need for a baby and was thankful for all the ladies had done.

Mama offered to drive her home after the shower. When they got to her apartment, Papa met them there to help unload. They got everything inside and Papa slipped out. Olivia looked at Mama in curiosity but she avoided eye contact. A few minutes later he came up the stairs pulling a large box. Olivia peered closer and realized it was a crib.

"Thank you, Mama! Thank you, Papa!" Olivia reached out and hugged them. Mama stiffened, but Papa hugged her tight and kissed her forehead.

"You get these things put away and I'll set it up," he offered. After a few hours, the nursery was in order. The little onesies were folded and placed in the drawers, cloth diapers in a basket under the changing table, a diaper pail on the floor and a crib full of blankets and sheets as well as a myriad of other baby necessities. Olivia walked Mama and Papa to their car and wandered back up to admire all the gifts she'd received. She couldn't believe her baby would be here soon.

Olivia decided to call Nonna and tell her about the baby shower. Nonna had her own surprise. "I bought an open-ended plane ticket. Once the baby is born, I'm coming up to stay with you for a few weeks. I don't want you to be alone until you feel like you've got the hang of things."

"Thank you, Nonna. I am so scared. What if I mess up?"

Nonna chuckled. "It's not what if, Olivia. You *will* mess up. It's all part of the process. The baby will be fine. You'll find out that they're tougher than you think." Olivia was relieved to know she'd have a helping hand.

Finding Hope

By the middle of September, Olivia was ready to be done being pregnant. The heat was making her miserable. Her feet were swollen, and her back was sore at the end of each day. All day sitting at a desk was like torture. She tried not to imagine what it would be like if she was married and spending her days at home instead of at work.

At childbirth classes, the husbands were so attentive to their wives that she couldn't help but feel envious. Lisa was wonderful, but she wasn't Jake. Not that Jake was that wonderful if she thought about it. He wasn't here with her and hadn't treated his wife right either. She now knew that life with the baby would be better with no man than with an unfaithful one.

Olivia rushed to her next doctor's appointment hoping that Dr. B would have some news for her and that labor was a few days away. Dr. B bustled in about a half hour late. She had been at the hospital for a delivery. She told Olivia about the new baby and the happy mama. Instead of feeling happy, Olivia felt jealous. What was wrong with her anyway? After Doc checked her, Olivia made eye contact with her hopes high. "Nothing yet, which isn't a surprise. You still aren't even to your due date."

"My due date is next Monday. How much longer could it be?"

Dr. B chuckled. This was a question she expected at the end of every woman's pregnancy. "I don't induce women unless they go two weeks over or, of course, if something is worrisome. Then we would get you in right away."

"You mean I could be pregnant three more weeks?" Olivia was dismayed. Dr. B patted her knee and reassured her that babies come when they are ready. "It feels like a long ways off, but you'll get there in no time."

As Olivia lugged herself to work, she had a pity party. When she walked in, Zig had some filing on her desk and Eric had notes for her to type up. She grumbled under her breath as she filed. Zig and Eric steered clear of her all day.

The next week when nothing happened, she snapped at Hope at Bible Study. When she shared it might still be a while, Hope tried to encourage her that the time would fly by. Olivia didn't mean to be grumpy, she was miserable. After the study was over, Lisa came up and gave her a hug. "I know how you feel, Olivia. I went a week over with mine. It's no fun at the end, and when it's hot, it's pure misery. I want to bring you dinner tomorrow. Ben told me I can stay and hang out for a while if that's okay?"

"That would be great!" Olivia felt so much better knowing she wouldn't have to pass another evening alone. Lisa showed up with a baked chicken casserole. She also had salad and homemade rolls. She wouldn't let Olivia lift a finger, and after dinner they decided to watch a few reruns of "I Love Lucy". Olivia had a wonderful time and was so thankful that Lisa took the time and effort to cheer her up.

The following week at her checkup, Dr. B shook her head to indicate it wasn't time yet. "My due date was yesterday, Doc. Is this baby *ever* going to come?"

"It'll be soon, Olivia honey. Don't get discouraged." She dreaded going back to Bible study to have her friends ask again what the doctor's report was. She didn't want to be cranky, but her emotions were all over the place. It was getting harder each day to stay positive. When she waddled in, no one but Lisa was brave enough to make eye contact; and even she didn't dare ask what the doctor had reported. Olivia decided they were afraid of her.

By the weekend, Olivia thought it was best that she lived alone. She wasn't sure what might happen if someone crossed her. All she knew is you don't mess with a woman past her due date! She wandered her apartment unsure of what to do with herself. She had washed and folded all the baby clothes, put the sheets on the crib and packed and repacked her hospital bag several times. She rubbed her hands over her stomach. "Come out, little one. Don't you want to meet mommy?" she begged. Maybe the baby was waiting on an invitation. She was ready to pull out the castor oil.

Olivia heard a knock on the door and almost ignored it. Most of the time when someone knocked on her door, it was kids in the apartment complex trying to sell something. *Well, at least it's a*

Finding Hope

distraction. She was thrilled when she opened the door and saw Hope, Lisa and Gina. Hope had a huge box of chocolate, Gina had a bouquet of daisies, and Lisa had a copy of The Ladies Home Journal and Good Housekeeping magazines. Olivia grabbed the box of chocolate, waved them all in, and plopped down on the couch. They all laughed. She told them she had microwave popcorn in the cabinet, but she wasn't sharing the chocolate. "This box will be empty by the time you leave!"

"I wouldn't dream of asking! Taking chocolate from a pregnant woman is like taking your life into your own hands!" Olivia nodded in agreement. She would've answered but her mouth was full. "So, have you thought of any names yet?"

Olivia swallowed. "I'm having a hard time with that. I think Adam if it's a boy, and maybe Joy for a girl? What do you think of those? Hope and Gina liked them.

"To know for sure if it's the right name, go to the bottom of the stairs and yell it a few times. If it feels comfortable then you know it's a good fit." Lisa always made her laugh. They talked for hours, and Olivia began to relax.

"I don't mean to be so testy, guys, but it has been so much harder than I thought it would be. I feel so impatient. I'm ready to meet my baby and move forward."

Hope nodded her head. "We understand, Olivia. You're in a tough situation, and we want you to know we are here for you in whatever way you may need us."

"Any time you want to bring me chocolate, that'd be fine." Olivia reached for another piece. They all laughed when she realized she'd eaten the last one already. "Oh my goodness, I've eaten the whole box! When I said that earlier, I was just joking."

They visited a few more minutes then had to get home. That night, as Olivia got ready for bed, she hoped one day she could help someone the way they had helped her. *Oh my. Next time not so much chocolate. My stomach hurts.* She was up and down through the night. She had already been uncomfortable, but the stomach ache from all the chocolate made things even worse.

The next day at work she couldn't get comfortable either. After a while, Zig poked his head out. "Are you okay, Olivia?" he said with concern.

"I'm fine, Zig. I have chocolatitus."

"Is it serious? Is the baby OK?" He was serious.

"Sorry. My attempt at humor. I ate a whole box of chocolate last night. Every time I think I'm starting to feel better, the pain kicks in again."

Zig let out a sigh of relief. "Well, take it easy. If you need anything let me know."

Olivia met Lisa and Hope for lunch. After she sat down, Lisa mentioned she appeared tired. "Eating that box of chocolate was a mistake." Olivia moaned and rubbed her hands over her stomach. Lisa eyed Olivia, scooted over and put a hand on her stomach as well.

"Does your stomach feel tight?" She gave Hope a knowing glance.

"I think so. I'm so mad at myself for eating that whole box! My stomach is still hurting at times."

"Why don't we time from the beginning of one pain until the start of the next and see what's going on." Lisa took off her watch and laid it on the table.

"You don't think I'm in labor do you?" Olivia stared at Lisa in surprise.

"It could be. Sometimes it's hard to tell at first." Olivia began to feel excited. Maybe it was going to happen at last! They all waited on pins and needles until the pain started again.

"That was six minutes. How long has this been going on, Olivia?"

"It woke me up at about two this morning, but it hasn't been that painful. I don't know."

They finished up and paid the bill. Lisa asked Olivia if she might be able to take off the rest of the afternoon and go for a walk. She called Zig and, with his permission, they all headed down to the river walk. For the next hour, they talked and walked, stopping every four to ten minutes for what they were now certain were contractions. Some were starting to hurt quite a bit, but so far

Finding Hope

Olivia was handling them pretty well. Olivia stopped to lean against a bench. "How long does labor last?"

"My sister took thirty-six hours for her first one!" Hope didn't know much about giving birth, but she had heard the story many times at family functions. Lisa nudged Hope to quiet her. She then saw that Olivia was terrified. "Not that it's how it will be for you, Olivia." Hope decided after that to keep quiet and let Lisa do the talking.

Olivia had to stop again to tie her shoe. As she bent down, she felt a gush of water. "Oh my word!" Lisa grabbed her arm to help her stand back up. "Your water broke! Thankfully the hospital is just across the bridge. Why don't we go get you checked out?"

By the time they got across the bridge, the pain had become quite intense. When they walked in, the receptionist behind the desk asked them a few questions. Olivia told her that she was ten days past her due date and her water had broken. A nurse was called to set up a delivery room.

"Wait!" Olivia looked at the nurse in fear. "I mean – are you sure? Maybe it's a false alarm. Don't those happen all the time?"

"Not once your water has broken. That's the point of no return." The nurse asked her questions as they walked down the hall. She got Olivia settled into a bed, and Hope tried to slip out. Olivia noticed and begged her to stay too. She wanted Hope on one side and Lisa on the other.

Dr. B arrived a few minutes later and congratulated her. "Sounds like it's baby time, Olivia. Let's check things out." Right then a strong contraction hit and Olivia cried out. Lisa stroked her forehead while Hope held her hand.

Doc waited for it to pass and then checked her. "Well, I'm surprised, Olivia. You're eight centimeters and 90% effaced. The baby is at a zero station. I'm not going anywhere, honey. You'll be ready to deliver this little one soon!" Olivia moaned as another contraction seized her. She began to feel terrified. *There's no way I can do this. I haven't even held a baby, let alone take care of one.* Doc ordered the nurse to bring in the delivery supplies, and the room began to bustle with activity in preparation for the arrival of her little one.

Olivia cried out during contractions and began to lose control. Doc came up next to her and held her face in her hands. "You listen to me, Olivia Martinelli. You are a strong woman, and you have handled a tough situation with strength and grace. You are going to be a mama today. Now take a deep breath and keep your eyes on me."

When Doc commanded, you listened. Olivia nodded her head, drew a breath and refocused. Hope and Lisa were at her side, and she tried not to let her fear overcome her. Doc decided to check her again and told her it was time to push. As Olivia drew in her breath and grimaced, she felt strength rise up in her and gave it all she had. For the next forty minutes, she pushed and prayed and cried and concentrated on one thing: experiencing the miracle of a new life. Soon the work was over, and she held a healthy baby girl! Doc congratulated her on a job well done while Hope and Lisa cooed at the baby.

"What are you going to name her?" Doc asked as she massaged Olivia's stomach. Olivia closed her eyes. "Joy. Her name is Joy."

The nurse helped an exhausted Olivia change into a clean gown, and get settled in her room. "Okay, Olivia, we've got you all cleaned up and there's still twenty minutes left before visiting hours are over. Are you up for visitors, or would you like me to walk them down to the nursery to see the baby?"

"Visitors?" Olivia wasn't sure who it could be. "Who would have even known I was here?"

"All I know is that there's a room full of people waiting to congratulate you. Is it okay for them to come in, or would you like them to come back after you've rested a bit?"

"No, go ahead and send them in." The nurse held the door open as Nora and Gina came in.

Nora rushed up to the bed. "I can't believe you're a mom!" Gina joined the others at the nursery window to see Joy.

Soon Gina, Zig and Eric came back to the room. "You did great, Olivia. She's perfect." Zig said as he set a balloon bouquet on the bedside table. She felt overwhelmed at the love and support her friends were showing. She couldn't help being amazed at God's goodness. What had seemed like such a hopeless situation had brought her such wonderful friends and a beautiful baby girl.

They stayed about fifteen minutes, and then the nurse cleared the room. "Thanks for coming everyone. Olivia has worked really hard and needs to rest." Olivia drifted off to sleep once they were gone.

The next afternoon she heard the sound of a knock on the door. "Come in,"

The door opened, and Olivia was pleased to see her mom and dad.

"Is this a good time?" Mama seemed uncomfortable to be there.

"Of course, come in. The baby is in the nursery. I'll call the nurses station and see if they can bring her back down." While Mama and Papa got comfortable, the nurses brought the baby to the room. When they handed her to Olivia, Mama got up to admire her. "Do you want to hold her, Mama?"

"Well, of course I do. She's my granddaughter."

Papa leaned forward to take a peek. "What'd you name her, Olivia?"

"Joy. It seemed like the perfect name."

Mama gave her full attention to the baby, while Papa asked how Olivia felt. He surprised all of them and asked if he could hold Joy. When he took her into his arms and peered down at her, he choked up. "She's the most beautiful baby I've ever seen." He stroked her cheek with his thumb.

Mama glanced at Olivia, and they shared a rare moment of pure happiness. "She *is* a beautiful baby. She looks a lot like you did when you were born." They stayed a short time, but when Papa handed Joy over to his daughter and new mommy, he promised he'd be back soon. He and Mama both kissed her cheek before they left to go home. Olivia felt more loved than she had in a long time.

A short while after her parents had left, Olivia heard another knock at her door. "Come in!.

Miss Elva poked her head in. "I heard there was someone here I need to meet."

Olivia broke into a big smile. "Come see her, Miss Elva. She's in the nursery during visiting hours, but you can go take a peek through the window." Miss Elva was gone longer than Olivia expected and when she returned she had tears in her eyes.

Miss Elva settled herself in the chair next to Olivia's bed. "What name did you decide on?"

"I named her Joy, but I can't think of a middle name. Nothing seems right. "

Miss Elva grew thoughtful. "Would you like to know how I've always chosen names?"

"Sure. Any ideas are welcome."

"You already know how I traveled with the ballet company when I was young. When I chose Clara's name, I had decided to pick names from my favorite ballets. After she died, I had pets. I decided to continue the theme."

"I'd be honored to carry on that tradition! Can you give me some ideas?"

"Well let's see. There's Coppelia, Odette, Clara, Giselle, Aurora and of course Juliet. Or you could use a famous ballerina's name. I suppose that would be acceptable." Miss Elva gave her a wink.

"Isn't there a famous ballerina with the name Anna?"

"Oh yes, Anna Pavlova." Miss Elva paused. "Joy Anna. A beautiful name for a beautiful baby. What do you think?"

"I like it!" Little Joy Anna woke up and made it known she was hungry so the nurse brought her to Olivia's room to be fed.

"I'll leave and give you some privacy, but you did just fine my girl. I'm so happy for you." She leaned and gave Olivia a kiss on the cheek before leaving her alone to feed the baby.

That evening as Olivia tried to get the hang of nursing, she began to feel nervous about going home. She even had to ask the nurses to help her change diapers, and they reassured her she'd be fine. She was catching on, but Olivia began to doubt everything everyone had been telling her.

She couldn't help but wonder if Jake somehow knew she'd had the baby. *Is he wondering how we are? If I am okay? Did he regret his decision to walk out on them?* Joy began to fuss, and Olivia held her close and began to coo at her. She quieted down in an instant, and Olivia realized no matter what happened, she loved this baby more than life and didn't need a husband.

Olivia tried to get some sleep, but the nurses were in an out often to check on them. Between that and feeding the baby, she was up most of the night.

Dr. B hustled into the room in the morning. "How's it going, Mama?"

"Wonderful, she's perfect, Doc! Did you see her little fingers? They're so sweet! She's darling!"

"Well, I'm glad you're getting along so well. Do you want to stay another night, or do you feel ready to head home?"

"Go home? Already?"

"Well, you can stay one more night if you'd feel more comfortable, but you do have to go home sometime." Olivia smiled as Doc laughed at her own joke. She opted to stay another night to learn more on how to care for baby Joy.

That afternoon, Lisa stopped by. She sat down on the bed next to her. "I wanted to let you know Brad asked about you. He wasn't sure if you'd want him to visit. I told him to give you some time to adjust to motherhood. But I thought you'd like to know he's thinking of you."

Olivia knew how hard it was for Lisa not to press and appreciated her sensitivity when she changed the subject. "I want to help you in any way I can. I know you're going at it pretty much alone, so you call me with any questions, okay?"

"I'm sure I'll be taking you up on that often." Olivia was thankful she had a friend she could count on. They visited a while and as soon as Lisa left, Hope arrived. Olivia had a night full of visitors. The next morning it was time to go home. Besides Lisa's generous offer, Olivia had one other comforting thought: *Nonna will be here soon.*

Chapter 12

Hope took Olivia and Joy Anna home from the hospital. She got Olivia settled on the couch and held the baby while Olivia rested.

There was a quiet knock on the door, and Hope answered since Olivia was still asleep. Nonna came in and Hope showed her the room Olivia had prepared for her. She then handed little Joy to Nonna and slipped out. When Olivia opened her eyes, Nonna was sitting next to her in a rocking chair with Joy. She sat up and grinned. "Isn't she beautiful, Nonna?" She nodded and kissed her little cheeks. Joy began to fuss, so Olivia fed her while she and Nonna visited. They talked about her delivery and decided to invite Mama and Papa for supper in a few nights.

Nonna was amazing. She cooked supper each night and doted on Olivia and the baby. The two weeks she was there flew by, and Olivia was so sad when the day came for her to go back home. Olivia knew she wouldn't see Mama and Papa much, other than the night they came for supper.

Nonna and Olivia sat on the couch talking when Nonna took her hand. "Olivia, I have something for you. I want you to take it and not argue with me about it."

Olivia laughed. "Sure, Nonna, I won't turn down a present!" She handed her an envelope. Olivia opened it and gasped. It was a check that was a little more than what she made in a year! "I can't take this, Nonna. It's too much!"

"Olivia, I have plenty. When Nonno died, he left me in a comfortable financial situation. Plus the shop sold for twice what I was expecting it to sell for. I have no mortgage or car payments. I have enough to spare. I *do* have one condition though." Olivia nodded at her and she pressed on. "I want you to stay home with Joy for one year. I know you can't do it forever, but I want you to take her first year and bond. It's so important. After the year, you can go back to work, but you'll not regret taking the time spent at home with her."

Olivia began to cry. How could she take such a large gift? Nonna placed her hand on Olivia's cheek, "*Tesoro*, if I couldn't afford this I wouldn't do it. Please swallow your pride and do this for me, for you – and most of all for Joy." Olivia was too choked up to speak. She nodded her head and hugged Nonna tight.

Olivia once again tried to express how much she loved her. "I don't know what I'd ever have done without you in my life, Nonna. You have been my biggest cheerleader for as long I can remember. I love you so much!"

As they waited for her cab to arrive, Nonna held Joy one last time while they planned for another visit around Christmas. The cab pulled up, and the driver loaded the luggage. As she waved goodbye, Olivia tried to hold back her tears until the cab was out of sight. It broke her heart to watch her one-in-a-million Nonna drive away.

Now it was Olivia and Joy – alone. She gazed down at her sweet, tiny little girl in her crib and tried not to feel scared. She decided to rest while the baby was asleep and laid down on the couch next to her car seat. She soon woke with a start when she heard little Joy crying and realized it was time to feed her. It was a lot harder at home than it was at the hospital when the nurses helped, but she seemed to have figured it out! The next few days, the main thing they did was sleep and eat. Lisa and Hope called each night, but no one stopped by.

Olivia knew she needed to tell Zig that she wouldn't be coming back to work after her maternity leave. Sooner was better than later. While Joy napped, she made the call. "Orban's Insurance, how may I help you?" asked a cheerful voice.

"Hi, can I please speak with Mr. Orban." It felt awkward to talk to her replacement.

"May I ask who's calling?"

"This is Olivia Martinelli." Olivia wondered if the woman even knew who she was.

"One moment please. I'll see if he's available."

Soon Zig's voice filled the line. "Olivia, how are you? We miss you around here!" He then miraculously lowered his voice. "I mean it, Olivia. We *really* miss you. Beatrice is a disaster. She can't keep up with the paperwork." Olivia smiled. It was good to be needed.

"That's why I'm calling, Zig. I'm not coming back after my maternity leave. My Nonna made it possible for me to stay home with Joy." She felt a wave of sadness hit her. She was thrilled to stay home with Joy, but she had loved her job. And she adored Zig and Eric.

Zig sighed. "I thought this might happen. I'm happy for you, Olivia, I really am. I just hate to lose you. You're the best assistant I've ever had. I'll tell you what. After that year is up, you call me. You'll always have a job here. You need only ask."

"I will, Zig. Thank you so much – for everything." They hung up, and Olivia let out the breath she didn't realize she'd been holding. She'd done it.

By the weekend, Olivia was feeling isolated but wasn't ready to venture out yet. She was so tired. On Saturday, Mama and Papa came over for a few minutes. Mama did her dishes while Papa held the baby. He was enchanted with Joy, and it delighted Olivia to see him so enthralled with her daughter. Mama didn't dote on the baby much, but it meant a lot that they came by to visit. She knew this was how they offered their quiet support.

Hope offered to pick Olivia and Joy up for Bible study, and she agreed. A chance to go outside and breathe in the fall air and see the rapidly changing leaves! Plus she was ecstatic to be around people! When they walked in the door, she glanced around the living room and her eyes stopped for a moment on Brad. He felt like his heart skipped a beat. He hadn't seen her in weeks.

"Congratulations, mom. Joy is amazing." His thoughts turned to Olivia: *She is beautiful. Motherhood suits her just fine.* Olivia knew he was having a reality check seeing her as a mother. She

Finding Hope

drew her attention back to those gathered around her sweet girl and felt wistful that Joy didn't have a father.

While Brad was teaching the lesson, he wished he could just talk with her. It was hard to focus on the lesson. He wanted to ask her how she was doing; if there were any needs he could help meet. He even wondered if the baby's father knew he had a daughter. Joy fussed a little at one point during the study, but everyone was patient and understanding.

They didn't get a chance to talk much during their snack time afterwards. Brad wanted her to settle in and not feel like he was waiting to pounce. He knew he needed to wait before he asked her out again, but he wasn't sure how long he could hold out.

On their way to Olivia's apartment, Hope said, "I wish I could be around more, Olivia. My art show is taking every spare second! As soon as it's over, I'll be here to lend a hand when I can."

"It's okay, Hope. We're doing well; getting to know each other."

As the weeks dragged on, Olivia grew more and more exhausted. She felt like she was nursing all the time. Joy Anna ate every few hours, and she didn't get much sleep. Lisa hadn't been able to stop by because her kids had been sick, so Olivia had no idea how normal it was to be so weary. She second-guessed each decision and felt like a terrible mother. By Sunday, she was a mess. Lack of sleep kept her home from church yet another week.

Several weeks passed by, and Olivia's loneliness intensified. Hope was neck deep in preparation for her first major art show, and once Lisa's kids had recovered from the flu, she came down with it herself. Nora hadn't stopped by once, and Olivia felt abandoned. With Joy eating so often and no one there to help, she was close to despair. She had been unprepared for the absolute exhaustion that comes along with a newborn. She didn't think to reach out to ask for help.

By the time Lisa was able to make it over to check on her, Olivia was frazzled. She was convinced she was a terrible mother and had begun to have panic attacks when Joy cried out of hunger.

"Olivia, are you okay? You don't look so great." Olivia dropped on the couch and began to cry. She couldn't talk at all. Lisa sat next to her and rubbed her back until she calmed down.

"I can't do this, Lisa. I'm so tired. What's wrong with me? When she cries I feel like crying. It hurts to feed her, and I can't ever sleep because she has to eat so often."

Lisa picked up Joy and watched Olivia in concern. "Olivia, I want you to go take a shower and get refreshed. When you come down, we'll figure this out."

After the shower, they settled on the couch with a cup of tea. Olivia apologized. "I'm sorry to melt down, Lisa. Even taking a shower helped. I guess I need more time to adjust."

"I think being a single mother has got to be pretty overwhelming. I know you don't have anyone to give you a hand. You may need to consider going to formula. Joy would sleep longer, and you'd get more rest and begin to feel more like yourself. Plus Hope or I could help with her feedings."

Olivia got up and walked to the kitchen without a response. She washed her dishes and vacillated between the benefits of each type of feeding. She knew how convenient nursing was for the baby and her budget, and she didn't want to quit because it was difficult. But she also knew herself and knew something needed to change. She walked back out to Lisa.

"I know I need help. You're sure she would sleep better on formula?" She and Lisa talked for a while and then decided she'd try it. Joy woke up and cried to eat, so Olivia picked her up.

"While you feed her I'll go shopping. When I get back, I'll sterilize the bottles and you can go sleep. I'll try to give her a bottle at her next feeding." Olivia finished feeding Joy while Lisa was gone. When she got back, she sent Olivia straight to bed. Olivia woke up and felt like a different person. She had slept for three hours! She shuffled downstairs and was beyond thankful to see Lisa holding Joy with an empty bottle next to her.

Olivia's eyes lit up. "She drank it?"

"Every bit!" Lisa showed her how to mix the formula and sterilize the bottles then headed back home after Olivia got the hang of it. The next week she got more sleep and began to feel

Finding Hope

human again. She decided to go to Bible Study that Tuesday, since she felt so much better. As she settled into the couch and snuggled Joy, Brad sat down next to her.

"How are you doing, Olivia? We've missed you the last few weeks."

"I'm doing better. I wasn't getting much sleep and got a little irrational. Thank goodness for Lisa!"

Brad leaned over to inspect Joy and reached out to touch her fingers. "Would you mind if I held her?"

"Of course not!" Olivia placed Joy in his arms. He gazed down and began to coo at Joy, and Olivia sat back on the couch and made eye contact with Hope. Olivia gave her a shake of the head. Brad was being kind, that's all. He gave Joy back and everyone gathered together for the lesson. On the way home, Hope teased Olivia about Brad's interest, but Olivia knew he was only being nice.

Olivia spent much of her time at home reading her Bible and drew even closer to God. Since Joy arrived, Scripture had come more alive to her. She began to depend on Him in new ways. After church, she began the habit of eating at Ben and Lisa's with several others from Bible study and started to feel like she was a part of the group. She felt more comfortable around Brad especially. That awkward phase had passed, and she knew they could be friends.

They all sat out by the campfire that night in Ben and Lisa's backyard. She and Brad were talking and laughing when Joy began to cry. Olivia didn't notice that Brad's eyes followed her when she got up to go feed her. Lisa saw though, and smiled to herself.

Olivia began to spend much of her free time with Lisa while Ben was at work. She often stayed for supper. She would play with all the kids while Lisa cooked. One evening, Olivia sat on the floor playing with James and Nicole when their doorbell rang. Lisa ran to answer the door because Olivia was too busy laughing at James' antics to hear the bell. "Hi, Brad, come in. I have to run to the kitchen and stir the soup, but the kids are in the other room if you want to go say hi."

"Oh no, I just wanted to drop this book off I borrowed from Ben. I'm sorry. I figured you'd already be done with supper."

Lisa laughed. "Oh sure, Brad. You *happened* to stop by at six when we always eat supper. Come in. I know how you starving single men try to get a home cooked meal any way you can!" Brad chuckled and came in. "Go in the living room while I finish up. Ben should be here any minute."

"Ben's not here? I'll wait on the porch. I don't want to give anyone a reason to gossip."

"Don't worry. Olivia's in the living room with the kids. It won't be just us." Lisa smiled. *Sometimes he's so uptight.* She pushed him towards the living room. "Go. I'll be in there in a few minutes. I have to get the rolls out of the oven." She tried to hide her grin but Brad caught it.

"Don't say a word, Lisa. She's not ready," Brad warned. He didn't want to scare Olivia off, especially since she seemed to feel comfortable with him again.

"I know, Brad, I won't. I promise!" With that Lisa returned to the kitchen.

Brad walked into the living room and James and Nicole launched themselves at him. "Mr. Brad, Mr. Brad!" James cheered as Brad tossed him in the air.

Olivia pretended to be hurt. "Well, I guess I know where I stand around here. As soon as someone new comes in, you forget all about me!" She and Brad laughed while James and Nicole ran back and forth, excited to have people to play with them. Joy woke up and began cooing and smiling at the kids. They were enthralled with her.

Olivia and Brad talked for a while until Lisa called them all to supper. They had a nice night together. Olivia was disappointed when it ended but knew she needed to leave so Ben and Lisa could get the kids in bed. Brad offered to drive her home so Lisa wouldn't have to go back out. She missed the mischievous look Lisa gave him as they walked out the door. When they got back to her apartment, Brad carried Joy's car seat to the door and wished her a goodnight. Olivia walked in and thought nothing of it.

Now that Joy slept through the night, Olivia felt like a new person. She grew to love being a mother more each day. She and Joy took long walks in the morning, and at lunch she ate on her front doorstep. She wanted to take full advantage of the blazing October colors and the crisp fall air. In the afternoon, one-month-old Joy napped while she read her Bible and worked on turning her little apartment into a home. She enjoyed the solitude while she worked on a cross stitch project for the baby's room and listened to her favorite instrumental tape. When she heard a knock at the door, she jumped up to answer it and was puzzled to see her dad on the doorstep. "Come on in Papa. Is everything alright?"

"I wanted to check on you is all." They were interrupted by the sound of Joy's crying.

"I'll be there in a minute, Papa. Let me go get her – come on in." She walked down the stairs with Joy and saw Papa's eyes light up. Papa reached out his arms for the baby and Olivia saw right through his excuses. Papa had fallen head over heels for her sweet girl. "Could you hold her while I clean up a little?" She hummed while she cleaned and listened to Papa talk to Joy. Sometimes she felt like she had more than she ever deserved.

Chapter 13

That Sunday, Pastor Dave preached about forgiveness. He shared about the danger of bitterness that grows in a heart that's unwilling to forgive. He told a story about a man who was angry and refused to forgive someone who hurt him; how that man put himself in a prison of bitterness and pain by his refusal to let go of his hurt and turn to God for healing.

"When you don't forgive, it affects you and you alone. Many times the person who's hurt you is either unaware of or doesn't care about the pain they've caused you. In the end, the person you hurt by holding a grudge is yourself."

Olivia was tuned in the whole sermon, and after the service declined the usual invitation to go to Ben and Lisa's for lunch. When she got home, she fed Joy and then decided to go for a walk. At the river, Olivia sat on the bench she had spent so many hours on with Jake. She knew what pastor had shared was true. She was angry that Jake had spent so much time wooing her. He convinced her he loved her, pressured her to give more than she was ready to give, and when she gave in and became pregnant, he disappeared from her life. It was unfair and it hurt.

"Oh Father, please help me to forgive Jake and move on once and for all. Please forgive me for my sin of involvement with a married man. Help me to let this go, and change me into who you want me to be." A simple but powerful heartfelt prayer. It was as if an incredible burden fell from her shoulders, and she knew she had done the right thing.

Tuesday night at Bible study she shared with her friends how much the sermon had meant to her. "I never thought about how I was wrong to withhold forgiveness." Brad decided that they would spend time in prayer, instead of the lesson he'd planned on sharing. It was an amazing night, and Olivia found herself once again praising God for this special group He had given her.

The following weekend was Hope's art show. Olivia was so excited to see her work. Hope had refused to let them see her studio. She insisted that she wanted them to see things in the right lighting with the pictures captioned.

Papa had come to watch Joy so that Olivia was able to dress up and go by herself. She walked up to the studio the same time as Brad and noticed how handsome he was in his suit and tie. When he opened the door for her, she sighed. *I wish things were different. He is such a wonderful man.*

They walked in and Olivia gasped. She couldn't believe how Hope so skillfully caught things on camera. While she and Brad wandered through the gallery, one particular picture enraptured her. It was a picture of a broken down wall. There were shards of glass and debris all around it, and the entire landscape was covered in dirt. The sky was cloudy, but the sun was shining through the clouds down onto a little daisy growing out of the rubble. The caption below it read: *"Beauty from Ashes" – Isaiah 61:3.*

The picture moved Olivia, and she stood there for a long time. When Hope came by to say hello, Olivia asked her where she'd taken the picture. Hope told her about a mission trip she'd taken to a little village in Haiti a few years ago. She shared about how the deep poverty of the people broke her heart. She had no idea how one mission team could bring relief. That afternoon while in town with the team, she saw that wall with the flower growing in the midst of total destruction. It had struck her how God could grow these beautiful people amidst the poverty and pain all around them. Olivia was thoughtful. "You captured it. Hope." She gave her a quick hug so Hope could mingle with her other guests.

Brad came up next to her to see if she was ready to go. He offered to give her a ride home so she wouldn't have to walk. "I'm fine. It's a few blocks away."

"I'd feel a lot better if you'd let me, Olivia. It's dark now and I'll be nervous for your safety." Olivia agreed to ride with him. Somehow at the bottom of the steps in the parking garage Olivia tripped, but Brad caught her arm before she fell.

Their eyes met as he reached to steady her. He had her arm in his hands, and they stood still. She felt a shiver go through her and broke eye contact. Brad cleared his throat, and they walked to the car in silence. When they got inside, they discussed Hope's art and shared about what pieces impressed them most.

It was a quick good-bye once they arrived at her apartment. Before going inside, Olivia sat on her front steps a while. She knew she could have feelings for Brad but also knew he had moved on. She felt like a moonstruck teenager for gushing over him when he kept her from a fall on the steps. *Ugh! I made a complete fool of myself!* She got up in disgust and hustled inside to see Papa and her baby girl.

Brad sensed that Olivia was more open to him than she had been. He hoped the right time would come soon, and he could begin to get to know her better. He knew patience was important, but he also felt as if God had given him a nudge and it was okay to try again. He had spent quite a bit of time with Ben the past few weeks, and they had prayed and prayed about the possibility of his and Olivia's relationship. If she knew how special she had become to him, she would have been surprised!

The following Sunday, Pastor Dave preached on love. He read a Scripture Olivia was unfamiliar with. It was in 1 Corinthians chapter 13. "Love is patient, love is kind. It does not envy, it does not boast, it is not proud. It is not rude, it is not self-seeking, it is not easily angered, and it keeps no record of wrongs. Love does not delight in evil but rejoices with the truth. It always protects, always trusts, always hopes, and always perseveres. Love never fails." God opened her eyes that what she and Jake had was nothing like this love God spoke of. She saw the areas she lacked in as well. *If God brings a man into my life again, I will learn how to love His way.*

At Bible study, Joy was fussy so Olivia took her out on the porch. She rocked her and enjoyed the last of the fall color. Later on the door swung open, and Brad stepped out to join her. He sat down on the steps and turned to face Olivia. "I want you to know that I am still interested in spending more time with you, Olivia. I want to respect your wishes, and I promise I won't ask again if you're uncomfortable. But I hope you'll give me a chance." Olivia was overwhelmed. "I'm sorry if this is awkward. I don't want it to affect our friendship if you're not interested."

His hopeful expression melted her heart, and Olivia found her voice. "Brad Parks, I *want* to spend time with you, too. I'm so glad you asked again."

He asked if she and Joy wanted to go on a picnic after church Sunday at the Riverwalk. Olivia agreed. He offered to pick her up before church so she didn't have to walk. "That sounds perfect, Brad. What kind of sandwiches do you like?"

"Nope, I asked you. I'll pack the lunch." Olivia was taken aback but thought it was sweet that he wanted to make lunch for her. They settled the details and joined the others back inside. Hope and Lisa both had grins that told her they knew what had happened. Olivia peeked up at Brad and he had a huge smile, too. She couldn't believe he was so happy to spend more time with her!

In the car on the way home, Hope demanded details. When they got into her apartment, Hope waited inside while Olivia fed Joy and put her pajamas on. Once she laid her down, she ran down the stairs for some serious girl talk. Several hours later they realized it was after one in the morning.

"I could talk all night, Olivia, but I have to meet a buyer at the studio at ten in the morning. Before I leave, though, can we pray?" Olivia nodded and bowed her head.

"Dear Jesus," Hope prayed, "Please be with Olivia and Brad as they begin this relationship. Help them to put the other as more important than themselves, help them to stay pure and give them wisdom on where you want this relationship to go. We thank you that you love them more than I ever could. Amen." They gave each other a hug, and then Hope had to get home.

After Hope left, Joy woke up to eat. Olivia prepared her bottle and hurried upstairs. She picked Joy up and sat in the rocking chair that Papa had brought over. She watched her little face relax as she drank and drifted back to sleep. She had on fuzzy terry cloth pajamas and smelled of baby lotion. Olivia snuggled her on her shoulder and breathed in the sweet baby fragrance. As they rocked, Olivia prayed for her girl. "God please protect my little girl as she grows up, and please use her in mighty ways for your kingdom." They rocked a long time before Olivia's eyes grew heavy with fatigue, and she laid her in the crib and staggered to her own bed.

On Thursday, Olivia decided to walk to Lisa's to hang out while the kids played. When she got there, Lisa had garbage bags sitting all over her living room, and her hair was a mess. "What's going on, Lisa?"

"I'm going through all the kid's clothes now that the seasons are changing. They've outgrown most of their winter clothes from last year, so I have to sort what to keep and what to donate. It's such a hassle."

"How can I help?" Olivia plopped down on the floor next to her. Lisa put her to work, and they sorted for quite some time until Lisa got up to go check on the kids upstairs in the playroom. When she left, Olivia stood up to stretch her back and then heard a shriek.

Olivia dashed up the stairs to see what happened. When she got to the top she saw it – a trail of long golden curls down the hall to the playroom. As she walked down to the door, she saw Lisa standing in silence peering down at little James and Nicole.

"Did I do a good job, Mommy?" James asked. "You said it was time to go for haircuts this week, but we saw how busy you were with our clothes and wanted to help. Now we can stay home. Isn't that great, Mommy?"

James had chopped about eight inches off of Nicole's beautiful hair. It would need to be fixed by a stylist and turned into a short bob to fix the uneven job he had done. When Nicole turned around Olivia gasped. James had cut her bangs, too! All the way to the top of her forehead! James and Nicole stared up at Lisa and Olivia's amazed faces and began to look unsure.

Lisa began to laugh, then Olivia did too. James, not one to miss an opportunity for fun, joined in and so did Nicole. When Ben got home, he jogged up the stairs to see what was going on. He took it all in: the hair, James with a pair of scissors in his hands, and sweet Nicole with her butchered tresses. He then turned to Lisa, bewildered. She stood on her tiptoes, kissed him and grinned. He and Lisa gazed into each other's eyes, able to communicate without words.

"Okay, kiddos, let's go downstairs and let mommy and Miss Olivia clean up. We'll also have a talk about scissor safety." Ben scooped the kids up and galloped down the hall as they cheered.

Olivia was impressed. "Wow, Lisa, you guys are so great. My parents couldn't have handled that without angry words. You're wonderful parents!"

Lisa shared how her own parents had been so fun. They loved to spend time together, were creative when they disciplined, and were careful not to do it in anger. "I knew I wanted a marriage like theirs and to parent with a similar style, they were so laid back – and we enjoyed being a family."

"Well, you've done it, Lisa. You guys have what I dream of having someday."

Lisa stopped sweeping for a moment and seemed to read her mind. "Olivia, you'll have it, too. Brad isn't the type of man to play with your heart. He's serious about you or he wouldn't have asked you out and then waited months until you were ready. I've known him five years now. He did date one other girl last fall, but she was awful. It didn't last long. He's always made it clear he wouldn't take a girl out unless he was ready to commit." Olivia didn't expect anything less. "I'm not saying he has a ring picked out or anything," Lisa joked. "But I do know you can trust him."

"Thank you. I know he's not one to lead me on, but it means a lot to hear someone else say it. I can't help but wonder, though, why me?"

"You know that verse in Isaiah 61 about God making beauty from ashes and giving strength for tears? That's what God does. He takes rotten situations and, if we wait and allow Him to change us, he turns them into something beautiful. That doesn't mean the situation was right, but He can bring good from it. It's another picture of what's called redemption." Olivia was awed that Lisa used the exact same verse that had touched her so much at Hope's art show. It seemed He was trying to show her He could redeem her lousy choices.

The next Sunday, Olivia was excited to go on the picnic with Brad and wanted to contribute something. She remembered the trunk Nonna had given her and descended downstairs to find a few things to take along. When Brad arrived, she was pleased to have her own little surprise for the picnic. They chatted about the verses that Olivia was learning to love in Isaiah, and Olivia shared about what Lisa had told her about them.

When they got to church, Brad carried Joy in for her, and Olivia walked beside them. She wondered if this was what it felt like to be a family, and then pushed the thought from her mind. She didn't want to rush anything. Joy was quiet through the service so Olivia was able to relax and listen.

Lisa noticed when Brad and Olivia walked in together and smiled. Several of the older ladies had taken note and she had no doubt that the prayer chain would be in full force this afternoon. Ben leaned over "You think this'll be on the prayer chain before service is over?" Lisa stifled a giggle as they stood for the first hymn.

This was Communion Sunday, and Pastor Dave spoke on "The God of Redemption". *Thank you, Lord,* Olivia kept thinking throughout the message.

The weather was perfect for the picnic. The grass was still green and the sky blue. The sunshine streamed through the puffy, cumulus clouds. The trees had lost their leaves, and they knew this would be one of the last nice days before winter. They chose a pleasant spot underneath the bare branches of an oak tree a few yards away from the river.

While Brad ran back to the car to get the picnic basket, Olivia set the table. She pulled her bag out from the stroller and found the antique ivory linen tablecloth with little orange and red leaves embroidered around the edges. Next she pulled out the clear glass milk bottle and filled it with water. Then she placed a sunflower from her garden in the bottle. She set the table with Nonna's clear orange glass dishes and goblets. She folded the napkins and sat down as she saw Brad heading back.

Brad was pleased that she had gone to so much trouble to make the table pretty for them. "I don't think my lunch is fit for this setting, Olivia," Brad joked as he pulled out ham and cheese sandwiches, chips, applesauce cups and a bottle of iced tea.

Olivia inspected the lunch he'd packed. "I think it's perfect!" They sat and talked for hours, and Joy waved her hands and feet and made happy baby noises until she drifted off for her afternoon nap.

Once they returned to Olivia's apartment, Brad helped her carry the baby and her picnic basket to the door. He stayed outside while she stepped in to set Joy down and put the basket on the table. She returned back to the door, and he explained that he didn't want to put either of them in a situation that could compromise his desire to remain pure. "I made a vow to stay pure until I'm married, and I want to honor you also." Olivia was so thankful that he was a man of such integrity.

"Thank you. You don't know how much that means to me." As she waved good-bye, she marveled at the difference she felt being honored in that way.

The following weekend, Olivia decided to invite Ben and Lisa, Hope, and Brad for dinner. She wanted to thank them for all they'd done for her. She wasn't a great cook, but she decided to try a chicken and rice casserole like Lisa had made for her before Joy was born. She also made a salad, and some heat-and-serve rolls.

She had fun preparing and setting the table with her linens and dishes from Nonna.

When everyone arrived, the girls kept complimenting Olivia over the gorgeous vintage tablecloth. It had flowers around the scalloped edges and a pretty bouquet in the center. The colors were deep blues and greens. She had several cobalt blue votive holders and vases going down the center of the table, with ivory votives and white mums in the little vases. Her plates were the same shade of blue. She had a quiet instrumental tape playing, and the aroma of the food cooking was mouth-watering. While they waited for the casserole to finish, Olivia told them about Nonna and how she had owned a little antique shop for fifty-one years before she sold.

"She had me go through her stuff and fill a large trunk to the brim with dishes and linens. She still has tons at her house, but she couldn't bear for any of it to go to strangers," Olivia explained as she ushered them to the table. The timer buzzed, and they all found a seat. Olivia asked Ben to pray, and then they began to eat.

They all dug in and as soon as she began to chew, Olivia panicked. The rice was crunchy, *very* crunchy. What had she done wrong?! She glanced over at Brad, and he was switching from the casserole to the salad. Suddenly he began to spit food onto his plate. "Glass," he sputtered. "I bit into a piece of glass!"

Olivia was horrified. She must have chipped the bottle of dressing when she tapped it on the edge of the salad bowl. Then her smoke alarm sounded. "The rolls!" she shouted as a burnt smell permeated the room. She jumped up to pull them from the oven, as Ben and Brad rushed to open the windows. Lisa grabbed the pan of rolls and set them outside to get the smoke out of the room. They all stood there in amazement, then began a loud chorus of laughter. Lisa put her arm around Olivia and joined in. Soon they were all gasping for breath from laughing so hard.

They decided to order pizza and play charades. It was a great time in spite of the rough beginning. When it was time to leave, Lisa offered to cook the next time and the laughter started up again. Olivia wholeheartedly agreed. "For the sake of our health and well-being, that would be best. I'm just glad none of us had to go to the ER tonight!" As they left, Lisa hugged her and whispered

Finding Hope

that she'd teach her how to cook if she wanted. Olivia nodded grateful for the opportunity to learn and hugged her back.

She and Brad sat outside on the steps and gazed at the stars. "I'm so sorry, Brad! I never learned to cook. My mom was always in a hurry after work and didn't want me underfoot while she made dinner. I wanted to make a nice meal, but that didn't go quite as planned." Brad chuckled and told her he still had a nice time.

"You'll have plenty of opportunities to practice, and I'd be glad to be the taste-tester. I *do* have good health insurance as well!" They laughed some more, and he gave her a quick hug. They were reluctant to say good-bye, but it was getting chilly, and she didn't want Joy to catch a cold.

Before Olivia knew it, it was a week until Thanksgiving. She wasn't sure what she would do this year. Mama and Papa had gone to visit Nonna, but she didn't want to take Joy on a plane yet and had decided to stay home. At Bible study, Lisa asked what the group's Thanksgiving plans were. It turned out that everyone's family was out of town, so she invited them all to her and Ben's house.

As they talked about who would bring what, Olivia wondered what on earth she could contribute. *Maybe a can of cranberry sauce? That's safe!* Lisa interrupted her thoughts, "Olivia, would you decorate? I'm terrible at it and you have such a gift!" Olivia agreed, happy to help in a non-cooking area. Brad was holding Joy, while Olivia planned with the girls. Every time she peeked at them over her shoulder, her heart beat a little faster. Seeing him care for her daughter was so romantic.

When she bundled Joy up in the foyer, Brad stepped over and helped her with her coat. When she turned to thank him, he was gazing down at her. "Olivia, I'd like nothing more than to kiss you right now. I know once we start down that road it's easy to get carried away." Olivia blushed and Brad continued on. "I wanted you to know how I feel. The reason I haven't' kissed you has nothing to do with my desire. It has to do with respect for you and obedience to God." As much as she wanted to be kissed by Brad,

Olivia was thankful he was a patient man. They settled for a hug, knowing that the kiss would come soon – in God's timing.

Olivia trekked to Lisa's each afternoon as they prepared for Thanksgiving. She taught her how to make rolls, and Olivia was thrilled when they pulled them out of the oven not burned! They shopped for the food, and Olivia helped her clean a few days beforehand.

On Wednesday, Ben took the kids out for the evening so Olivia and Lisa could set the tables and decorate. After thinking about taking them to the Pizza Palace where they could play games, he decided he didn't want to try that without another pair of hands. He settled on drive thru cheeseburgers and a trip to the Farm and Family store. The kids could pet the puppies and he could pick up the drill he'd been eying.

By Thursday morning, Olivia felt like a homemaking pro. She was in the kitchen again with Lisa. It was her first time using the *Snugli* she'd been given at her baby shower. Joy was happy and her hands were free. They made stuffing and mashed potatoes while they waited for the turkey to finish.

When the doorbell rang, Lisa and Ben were in a discussion on how to carve the turkey, so Olivia went to answer the door. When she opened it, Brad was standing there with a green bean casserole. He grinned when he saw Olivia in her apron, her cheeks red from rushing around in the kitchen. He leaned down and kissed her cheek. "Happy Thanksgiving, Olivia." Olivia blushed. She hadn't expected that. They walked in together, and Brad took Joy while Olivia and Lisa put the final touches on the table. Soon after everyone else began to arrive, the mood became festive. They prayed and then feasted on the wonderful meal. Brad and Olivia sat next to each other, and she could tell things had grown deeper between them.

After supper, the men relieved the women and did all the clean up. The ladies sat in the living room and visited while they took turns holding six-week-old Joy. James and Nicole basked in all the attention, and Olivia felt very content. When clean up was done,

Finding Hope

they played games until late in the night. By the time Olivia got home, it was far too late to call Nonna to wish her family a happy Thanksgiving. She called first thing the next morning. She was excited to tell Nonna about Brad kissing her cheek.

"I can't wait to meet this one, Olivia. He seems like the real deal."

"He is," Olivia gushed. After a few minutes, Nonna passed the phone off to Mama.

"Hello Olivia, we missed your call yesterday." Olivia had known her mom would be upset about the missed call. *I should've talked to Nonna last and ended on a good note.*

"I'm sorry Mama. Things were crazy at Ben and Lisa's with all those people there, but we had a nice time. How was your Thanksgiving?"

"It was fine, I had hoped to spend it with the whole family. We won't be around forever you know." Mama always managed to sneak in a guilt trip or criticism. Olivia knew it would happen, but just once it would be nice to have a pleasant conversation.

"I am sorry, Mama. Is Papa there?"

"No, he realized we most likely wouldn't be hearing from you and went downtown for a while. I guess we'll see you when you get home. Happy Thanksgiving." With that they hung up.

That afternoon while Joy napped, Olivia decided to decorate for Christmas. She didn't have a lot to decorate with, so she ventured outside with a pair of scissors. She cut some branches down from the evergreen trees surrounding the parking lot and made swags to hang around the windows. She then dug a beautiful red tablecloth out of her trunk and put some pinecones she had gathered in a sparkling crystal bowl in the center of the table. On either side she placed Nonna's beautiful silver candlesticks with white tapered candles. She had hoped she could get a tree, too, but it still felt festive with the little she had been able to do. That evening the phone rang, and it was Brad. "I'm going to get my Christmas tree tomorrow. You two want to come along?"

"Well, I can't speak for Joy, but I'd *love* to." Olivia was feeling more and more comfortable around Brad.

The next morning, she bundled Joy and walked to the hardware store a few blocks away. She bought a few boxes of colored lights and loads of tinsel. She remembered she needed a tree stand, so she picked that up as well. When they got home, she laid Joy down and made a thermos of hot chocolate and packed some coffee mugs in a picnic basket. Then she decided to make a batch of the chocolate chip cookies that Lisa had walked her through a few days ago. When Brad arrived, he carried the basket and car seat to the car while she ran upstairs to wake up Joy.

Olivia's family had always put up an artificial tree. Mama didn't like the mess the needles made. She was delighted when they arrived at the tree farm and she saw the horse and sleigh at the entrance. They got out of the car and Brad helped Olivia up to her seat on the sleigh and passed Joy to her. The snow fell all around them as the sleigh pulled them to the section of trees they were to choose from.

Olivia chose a short fat Douglas fir and Brad chose a taller one. They laughed as they rode back on the sleigh and realized there was no room for both trees on top of the car. They took Brad's home first, and then traveled back for Olivia's. When they got to her apartment, they agreed that Brad shouldn't come in. They stood on the porch to say good-bye, and she could see the love in his eyes. "Maybe next year we'll need one Christmas tree for both of us."

"Maybe," Olivia said with a smile. "But whose place will we set it up at?" she joked. They laughed and exchanged a quick hug. As Brad drove away, hope welled up in her heart that maybe there would be a happy ending for them.

It was harder to set up a tree than Olivia had imagined. After a couple hours of struggle to get it to stand up, then putting on lights and tinsel, she wanted someone to show it to. It seemed funny to go to all that trouble for her and Joy.

"What do you think, sweetie? Will this do, or should I add more tinsel?" Joy watched the lights, and giggled when they twinkled.

"I guess you approve, huh? Now all we need is some presents." Joy smiled right on cue.

The weeks that followed were a flurry of activity as Christmas approached. Olivia agonized over what gift to get Brad. She called Lisa, but she wasn't sure what to do either. Things were getting more serious between them, and Olivia knew she was falling in love. It was so different this time.

She studied the verses on love that Pastor Dave had preached about in First Corinthians. They were being patient. Even though she felt a desire to hold his hand or kiss him, she knew their choice to wait protected them. She was full of hope instead of guilt. Brad was the least self-seeking man she had ever known. Then she had an appropriate gift idea. She called Lisa to see what she thought and she agreed. It was personal but not too forward either.

That weekend, their Bible study group went Christmas caroling, and afterwards they gathered at Ben and Lisa's for cookies and hot chocolate. Lisa took baby Joy so Brad and Olivia could go on a walk. They walked in amiable silence for a while. Then Olivia told him that Nonna was coming for a visit. "I can't wait for you to meet her, Brad. She is so special to me."

"I would love to, Olivia." They planned for a meal at her house the following week. "I won't turn down a meal at your house. It's bound to be an adventure!" Olivia was used to her cooking being an opportunity for humor, and she laughed – something she did a lot of lately when she and Brad were together. As they walked and talked, it began to snow again so they headed back. Brad wanted to get Olivia and Joy home before the roads got worse.

Chapter 14

Nonna arrived on Saturday, and Olivia decided to ask if she would go to church with them. Nonna agreed. She was thrilled that Olivia had found such peace, but was unsure what she thought of Christianity. They got ready Sunday morning, and Brad picked them up. He and Nonna talked like old friends. At church Lisa rushed up to meet her. She had been disappointed she didn't meet Nonna when Joy was born. They all decided to go to lunch one day before Nonna left.

The service was perfect. It was all about how God loves us and wants us to come to Him. Pastor shared about how God had made the way for us by sending Jesus Christ to earth to live. Nonna appeared thoughtful as they left, and Olivia decided not to press.

Brad came for lunch, and Olivia served soup and rolls. Nonna and Brad praised her efforts to learn cooking, and Olivia was elated that no one choked on glass and the rolls didn't burn! After Brad left, she and Nonna talked for hours. Olivia told her all about what kind of man he was, how he respected her and wasn't pushy. Nonna was excited for her and thought he was a wonderful man, even if he was a little uptight. They played with Joy and laughed over her attempts to talk back to them.

On Christmas Eve, they attended the church's candlelight service, and there, in the pew between Olivia and Brad, Nonna gave her life to Jesus. Olivia's heart overflowed with joy. She cried and hugged Nonna as the service ended. Brad put his arm around Nonna, too. When they got home, they decided Brad would come in the morning to do gifts with them and to meet Mama and Papa. Olivia warned him that Mama was tough, but he assured her it would be okay.

Olivia put the gifts around the tree and, when she woke up, Nonna had added hers, also. They worked in the kitchen together

Finding Hope

to make breakfast for everyone. Olivia heard a knock at the door and ran to get it. It was Mama and Papa. They came in, their arms full of gifts, and Nonna came out to kiss them. Mama looked uncomfortable, but didn't object. Olivia hadn't seen Mama allow Nonna to hug or kiss her before. Papa hugged them both and then snuck to get Joy from her playpen. Brad arrived a few minutes later and Olivia made introductions.

Papa and Brad sat at the table and talked while she, Mama, and Nonna brought the food out. After breakfast, they exchanged gifts, and Joy got the most by far. They all laughed that the Raggedy Ann doll Nonna had bought was bigger than Joy was. The afternoon progressed well, and conversation flowed without any awkward pauses. Olivia was so relieved that Brad fit in, and Mama and Papa seemed to like him.

When they left, Nonna offered to take Joy up for her nap so Brad and Olivia could exchange gifts. When Brad opened his gift, he saw the beautiful leather bound Bible with his name engraved on the cover. He was overwhelmed. "It's wonderful, Olivia. I love it. Thank you so much! My gift for you is in the car; come outside with me?"

They strolled to the car and he opened the back door. She peeked in and saw a car seat strapped in the back. "I don't plan on taking that out, Olivia. I want you and Joy to stay in my life."

Olivia lifted her hand to his cheek. "Brad Parks, you are the best man I have ever known." He put his hand on top of hers, and they stood still. She lowered her hand, but he didn't let go. He led her to the steps, still holding her hand in his.

"Olivia, I want to take you to meet my parents. I've told them about you, and I'd be honored if you'd come home with me in a few weeks." Olivia was speechless. She desired to take this step but was nervous to go meet them with a baby. What would they think?

"I want to meet them as well, Brad. Would it be wrong if we didn't take Joy this time? I want to give them a chance to meet me before they find out I have a daughter." Brad seemed to understand, but Olivia continued. "I want a chance for them to like me before they find out about my past. If they are disappointed after they find out, at least I'll know they would've liked me had I done things the right way."

Brad agreed. "I think its okay, Olivia. Do you have anyone who could watch her a few nights while we're there?" Olivia decided to check with Lisa, and they picked a weekend in January.

Later that evening, Olivia told Nonna about their conversation. "Olivia, I think he's fallen in love. I'm not surprised at all that he wants his parents to meet you."

"I know I love him, and it's so different doing things this way. I feel so treasured with him; like I'm a princess worth waiting for."

Nonna agreed. "That's how it was when Nonno and I courted. I sure wish times hadn't changed so much. That sure was the ideal way to do things." Nonna had to leave in the morning, but Olivia promised to call after she returned from meeting his parents.

Brad knew that once he called his mom and told her he was going to bring Olivia home, she would begin to plan a wedding. It had been that way for his brother, and she had been after him for several years to settle down and start a family. The phone rang several times, and he thought he had missed them. Just as he was about to hang up, his dad picked up. "Hello."

"Hi Dad."

"Brad! Good to hear your voice. Did you have a nice Christmas?"

"I did. I was able to celebrate with some friends from church, and we had a great time. Hey, could you have mom pick up the other phone? I want to talk to both of you."

"Sure thing, son. Hold on a second while I find her."

A few minutes later, he had both of his folks on the line. The long pause told them that Brad had something important to say.

"I would like to come home to visit in January and thought we could pick out a weekend."

"Oh, Brad, you had me worried for a minute. Is that all you needed? You know you can come home anytime."

"Well, I was curious if it would work for me to bring a guest. Her name is Olivia, and I'd like you both to meet her."

Finding Hope

Complete silence filled the line. Then they all began to talk at once.

"You found a girl!" his mom exclaimed.

"I did, Mom, and I think you're going to *love* her."

His dad hung up and let Brad talk to his mom. "I'll see you soon, son. We'll talk more when you get here."

His mom wanted to know all about Olivia. They talked for about a half an hour and picked a weekend for him to bring her home. "She must be special, Brad. I've always known it would take an incredible woman to catch your eye."

After they hung up, Brad's thoughts turned to Olivia. *Lord, please help my parents to see what a treasure Olivia is, and help her to feel welcomed.*

Olivia was a nervous wreck about meeting Brad's parents. She asked Lisa whether it was okay to *not* tell them about Joy at first. Olivia wasn't ashamed of Joy. She was ashamed of herself. Lisa understood and was excited to keep Joy for the weekend. "It's been a few years since we've had a baby around here. It will be fun!" Lisa tried to set Olivia's mind at ease. They were working on a recipe for ribs that Olivia wanted to try. She and Lisa were cooking together several times a week now, and Ben and Brad were benefitting greatly from this training!

Ben and Lisa had been wonderful to open their home for them to spend more time together. Olivia had gotten better at cooking, too, so that was a definite bonus! Lisa taught her how to read a recipe and how to plan meals. She taught her the simple formula her mother had taught her: choose your main dish, a vegetable and a starch. Once you learned to read a recipe, it wasn't that hard! Olivia still got nervous to cook on her own and relaxed more when Lisa was there.

The next weekend, it was time to go home with Brad. As Olivia packed Joy's bag, she hoped she was doing the right thing. She'd hadn't been away from Joy for more than an hour or two and was going to miss her. When Brad picked her up, Olivia was worried sick. "It's going to be alright, Olivia. They're going to love you!" Olivia tried to calm her nerves – she needed chocolate. Lisa ran out to the car to get Joy, and before she knew it they were on their way.

It was a six-and-a-half-hour drive to Brad's hometown in Kentucky, and they didn't get there until late. When they pulled up, it was a beautiful two-story home set back in the woods. The lights were shining through the windows, and it looked perfect to Olivia. Before they even got out of the car, Brad's mom had thrown the door open and rushed down the steps.

"Come in, come in! We've been waiting for you!" She grabbed Brad and hugged him, then reached for Olivia. Olivia was overwhelmed at such a warm welcome. It wasn't anything like she'd experienced before.

They stepped inside, and Brad's dad waved from the couch. "Get in here, Bradley. The game's about to start."

Mrs. Parks led Olivia to the kitchen. The table was next to a large stone fireplace, and she had tea and cookies arranged on a tray. "I'm so excited to get to know you, Olivia. My Brad has never brought a girl home for us to meet, so I know you must be special."

Olivia blushed. "I think your son is the most amazing man I've ever met, Mrs. Parks. I'm honored to be here with him." Mrs. Parks asked her how they met, and Olivia was able to share about Bible study and how she had come to the Lord last year. They talked about her hobbies and books they'd both read. By the time the football game was over, Olivia knew she'd love Brad's mom. They took drinks and snacks to the living room, and Brad's dad stood up to hug her.

"I'm sorry for my rude welcome, but the Steelers were on, and the Super Bowl is a week away!"

Olivia laughed. "Don't worry, Mr. Parks. My Papa is the same way." They talked for a while, then Mrs. Parks showed Olivia to the guest bedroom.

The next morning, Mr. and Mrs. Parks decided to stay home from church since they had such a short time together. Mrs. Parks made a huge breakfast and refused to let Olivia or Brad lend a hand. When Mr. Parks attempted to sit down, Mrs. Parks spoke up, "Not so fast B. G.! You're on pancake duty!"

Mr. Parks laughed and wrapped his arms around her and kissed her cheek. "Okay, okay, give me that spatula, woman." He whistled as he flipped pancakes while Mrs. Parks cooked bacon and eggs. Brad and Olivia drank their coffee and enjoyed visiting with them while they cooked.

When they sat down, Mr. Parks prayed and they dug in. The food was delicious and Olivia was stuffed. Mr. Parks did the dishes while Mrs. Parks put food away and washed down the table. Olivia had begun to see from watching Ben and Lisa, and now Brad's parents, that marriage could be wonderful. She glanced at Brad, and he seemed to understand what she was thinking.

They all headed out for a walk after breakfast. Brad showed her his favorite trails in the woods. One led to an old tree house that he and his brothers had built. "It's safe to go up. Do you want to see it?" Olivia decided to check it out and climbed up. Brad's mom and dad had walked a little further down the path to see the river.

Olivia laughed when they got inside. There was a hand-painted sign that stated: NO GIRLS ALLOWED. "Am I breaking any rules being up here, Brad?"

"My brothers brought their girlfriends up here, too. This is the spot where Brandon proposed to Sherry." Brad grabbed her hand and pulled her to him. He hugged her and held her for a minute, then he broke away and climbed out of the tree house. Olivia followed him down. "I'm sorry, Olivia, it's so hard not to kiss you, and sometimes I don't think I can make it another day."

Olivia agreed that it was difficult. "I'm so thankful for you, though, Brad. You're giving me a chance to do things right. You don't know how much it means to me." He reached for her hand again, and they walked back to the house. That afternoon they had to head back home so Brad could be at work on Monday morning. Brad's mom and dad hugged them good-bye, and Olivia was glad she'd been able to meet them.

Once she was home with Joy, reality set in again. She daydreamed, though, of life with Brad as she gave Joy her bath one morning. She couldn't believe his family and how easily they had accepted her. She knew even if they were disappointed about her being a single mom, that they liked *her*.

She spent the evening praying that they would at least accept Joy once they found out. She called Nonna after she rocked Joy to sleep and told her all about her trip. "They were wonderful, Nonna. It was like the family I've always wanted to be a part of. All the boys names start with a B. It's so funny!" Nonna was full of questions, and before long it was time to hang up. "I love you Nonna!"

"I love you too, Olivia. You're the bright spot in my life."

After Bible study, Brad told her in the car that he was calling his parents to talk and asked if it was all right to tell them about Joy. He could explain why they hadn't shared sooner. Olivia agreed it was best to tell them right away. They prayed together that God would go before them and were quiet most of the ride home. A few hours later her phone rang, and Olivia was sure it was Brad. "Hello?" She had been nervous to hear how the conversation went.

"Olivia? This is Mary, Brad's mom."

"Hi, Mrs. Parks." There was a pause. *Okay, here it comes.*

"Oh, Olivia, I *had* to call you. I wanted you to know if Brad loves you, we will too! We had a wonderful weekend with you and can't wait to meet little Joy."

Olivia began to cry. "Thank you so much! I'm sorry we didn't tell you right away. I was so nervous and ashamed of myself."

"Sweetie, people make mistakes, and sometimes those mistakes are what lead us into the Father's arms. You've turned to Him and received forgiveness, and I have nothing to hold against you." Mrs. Parks asked about Joy, and Olivia told her all about her precious baby. When they hung up, Olivia called Lisa to tell her the good news. Lisa was thrilled and they made plans to get together the following afternoon to talk more.

Finding Hope

    Wednesday Olivia visited Lisa, and they made a nice supper together. When the guys arrived, Ben asked her and Brad if they had any Valentine's Day plans. He and Olivia looked at each other and shook their heads.

    "Lisa and I have reservations set for Saturday night, not on Valentine's Day. If you want to drop Joy off so you can go out, we'd be glad to watch her." Olivia and Brad agreed and decided to go out for a nice dinner at Luigi's, Olivia's favorite Italian restaurant. She hadn't had a chance to dress up much since she'd had Joy, and it would be so romantic to go together. Brad planned to pick her up at 5:30 on Thursday at Ben and Lisa's.

    Hope called the morning of the date and asked if Olivia could swing by around 5:00 at the shop. She needed her opinion on a display. Even though she hadn't been able to pursue classes at the college, God was providing ways to use her eye for design. Hope agreed to pick her up and have her to Lisa's in time for her date with Brad. When they arrived at the studio, Hope carried Joy in. "I have to run in and grab a frame. Can you take a peek? The display is in the red room." Olivia made her way to the back of the studio. She blinked in surprise when she got there. Brad stood in the center of the room. "What are you doing here Brad? I thought we were going to meet at Ben and Lisa's after I dropped Joy off," Olivia asked in confusion.

    Brad took a step towards her and reached for her hands, kneeling in front of her. "Olivia Martinelli, you are the woman I've waited for my whole life. From the moment I first saw you, I knew you were the one. Will you marry me?"

    Brad Parks loves me, and he wants me to be his wife! Olivia had dreamt this moment would come, and the expectant look in Brad's eyes spoke volumes. "Yes!" she whispered, and Brad slipped the ring on her finger. "It's so beautiful, Brad!"

    He stood up and pulled her to him. "I love you, Olivia. I've waited months to tell you." Then he lowered his head and kissed her for the first time. Olivia had worried that this moment would be awkward, but it wasn't – it was perfect. Brad then led her to Hope's office, and she couldn't believe it! Mama and Papa were there, Mr. and Mrs. Parks, Ben and Lisa and their friends from

Bible Study and –"Nonna!" Olivia cried and ran into her arms. Nonna was beaming and admired her ring. "You've done well, Olivia. I couldn't be happier." Lisa demanded to see the ring, and they broke into laughter. Olivia and Brad were hugged and congratulated over and over.

The room cleared, and soon all that was left was family. "I made a reservation for *all* of us at Luigi's. We'll meet you there," Brad announced with a grin.

Once they reached the car, Brad opened Olivia's door before getting in. "I can't believe you did that, Brad. I don't think I've ever been happier!"

Brad reached for her hand. "I wanted it to be special. I have to admit, though, Hope and Lisa were the ones who helped with details."

Olivia laughed. Gathering all their friends and family to be there had Lisa's name written all over it. The restaurant staff congratulated them as they walked to the table, and it was a wonderful evening of celebration. On the drive home they decided on a June wedding. Neither of them wanted to wait much longer.

Sunday at church, Pastor Dave announced a women's conference that was coming up, and Brad whispered to Olivia that she should go. They talked about it after church, and Brad offered to keep Joy for the weekend. Olivia was hesitant.

"Olivia, if we're going to get married, I want Joy to be my daughter, and I need to spend more time with her. I can handle it." She reluctantly agreed, and they made plans for him to stay at her apartment while she was gone.

When Olivia told Lisa and Hope she could go, they signed up also and booked a room together. Sunday night the girls met at Flo's for coffee and a piece of Hank's famous apple pie. Lisa presented Olivia with a gift – a wedding planner. They opened it up and realized they were already a few months behind. The church was free the weekend they wanted, and Pastor Dave was honored that they asked him to officiate. Hope begged to do the photography as her gift, and Olivia was happy to accept. They chose a weekend in March to explore the dress shops, and Olivia was giddy with excitement.

The next night, Olivia and Brad rendezvoused at Ben and Lisa's to talk over more plans. They decided to ask Brad's brothers and Ben to be groomsmen. Olivia wanted to ask Lisa, Nora and Gina to be her bridesmaids. Hope couldn't be a bridesmaid since she was the photographer.

"Olivia, would you feel comfortable having everyone in the wedding over for dinner? She agreed, and they decided to go simple and have spaghetti, salad and garlic bread. "You should let them bring their own dressing to avoid any glass mishaps," Brad teased. They stayed late planning, and she told him that her and the girls were shopping for dresses in a few weeks.

"Mama called and told me that she wanted to come along when we shop for dresses, which made me really happy. God is answering our prayers for me to have a better relationship with her."

When Olivia called Nora to invite her for dinner, she hesitated. "I don't know, Olivia. I don't know any of them. Don't you think it would be awkward?" Olivia begged her to come, and she finally agreed. Brad's brothers couldn't come because of the long drive, but they were thrilled to be part of the wedding. Olivia couldn't believe how everything was falling into place, it felt like a fairy tale.

Chapter 15

Time sped by and soon it was March. Olivia was all packed for the weekend conference and was busy getting everything ready for Brad to take care of Joy. When he knocked on the door, she couldn't believe it was already time to go. He came in, and she showed him where things were and gave him the notes about Joy's schedule.

When they traipsed up to Joy's room, she was awake and playing in her crib with her stuffed animals. She reached her arms up for Brad. Olivia was amazed at Brad's love for her and Joy, and his acceptance of their situation. He picked Joy up and she laid her head on his shoulder.

As Olivia watched Brad with Joy, she lost even more of her heart to him. She couldn't wait until they had a home together and didn't have to be on guard. Brad handed Joy to Olivia and carried her bags down the stairs. They waited by the window for Lisa and Hope. When they pulled up, Olivia hugged Brad and kissed Joy good-bye.

The camp they were staying at was a few hours away, and there were several women speaking over the weekend. They were able to pick different workshops to attend, and Olivia chose three: one on the best start for your marriage, one on preparing healthy meals for your family, and one about growing in your relationship with God. Hope and Lisa had chosen different workshops, but Olivia was excited about the ones she'd chosen.

When they found their cabin and unpacked, Olivia realized Brad had tucked a note into her bag. Tears came to her eyes as she thought about how much God had turned her life around. Lisa, Hope and Olivia sat in a circle on the floor and talked until it was time for the first workshop.

Finding Hope

That evening, they were up late sharing what they'd learned through the day. Olivia was excited to be surrounded by women who wanted their lives to honor God. She hoped someday she could encourage younger women the same way. The next evening, she was able to call Brad to see how things were going. He told her all about what he and Joy were doing. He was having a great time and didn't seem frazzled at all. "Thanks for letting me stay with her, Olivia. It means a lot to get to spend some one-on-one time with her."

"Thanks for loving us, Brad. We are so blessed to have you in our lives. I never in a million years thought my life would turn out like a fairy tale after such a rocky start."

"Olivia, you are the most beautiful, kind, humble woman I know. I thank God every day that you walked into Bible Study that night. You are the love of my life, and I can't wait to start our life together." Olivia sighed. She wished they could be together now, but she knew it would be soon. They hung up with words of love, and Olivia couldn't sleep that night. She missed Brad and Joy. The next morning was the last day of the retreat. Although Olivia was glad she'd been able to go, she was even *more* glad to get home.

When she walked in the door of her apartment, it was tidy and lunch was ready. *I wonder if Brad even needed me.* Brad hugged her and told her Joy was out in the living room. When she leaned over to pick her up, she was thrilled. Joy's dress was on backwards! They *did* need her! She kissed Joy and headed back to the kitchen. After a gourmet lunch of grilled cheese and canned tomato soup, they visited a few minutes before Brad left.

He reached for her hand and asked Olivia what she was doing the next weekend. "I'm dress shopping with the girls."

"Well, I would like you to come hunt for houses with me," Brad said.

Olivia glanced up in surprise, "Do you really think we can afford to buy a house?"

"I have enough saved for a down payment. It won't be anything fancy, but it will be ours."

"Where do you want to look?"

"There are several starter homes for sale in Ben and Lisa's neighborhood. I thought it would be nice to live close so that you could walk to each other's houses to visit."

They decided to make an appointment with the realtor for the following Saturday.

Saturday morning Mama picked her up to go to The Bridal Boutique. They had decided to meet Lisa, Nora and Gina there. When they walked in, the stylist greeted them. "Hello, my name is Marianne and I'll be working with you today. Please come sit down and we can chat a little about what you're dreaming of. Then I'll pull some dresses."

Olivia followed her, excited to see what kind of dresses they had. They all sat around the desk while she questioned Olivia. "There are many things to consider for your dress. What style are you going for?" Olivia knew she wanted a simple, elegant, classic style dress; nothing too trendy.

"We'll need to see dresses in a cream color," Mama stated. "Olivia has already had a baby, so white is out of the question." There was an uncomfortable silence. Olivia was speechless.

"Is this how you feel, Olivia?" Marianne asked. Olivia shook her head and stood up.

"I can't do this." She walked out, leaving Mama and her friends in the salon.

She raced around the corner, found a little park and sat on a bench hidden behind some bushes. Doubts filled her mind, and she began to weep. *What was I thinking marrying Brad? I'm not good enough for him. I can't bear to shame him by pretending to be pure when I walk down the aisle. Everyone knows my past.*

She cried uncontrollably and determined she had made a mistake. Mama was right. Marrying Brad was a mistake. She sat there for a long time and then realized she had to get back home to Joy. When she walked back to the shop, Mama and her friends were gone. She waited at the bus stop, determined to talk things out with Brad when she got home.

When she opened the door to her apartment, she was nervous and broken-hearted. She had to face Brad since he had watched Joy for her. She walked to the living room and Brad jumped up from the couch and took her in his arms. Olivia began to cry again, and Brad stroked her hair.

"Lisa called me. I know what your mom did. We were worried sick about you." Olivia couldn't stop her tears, and Brad led her to the couch. "Olivia, look at me," he said in a strong voice. Olivia opened her mouth to explain. "No, I don't want you to say anything. Listen first." Olivia nodded her head.

"I know where you're mind is going, and let me say that I love you with every ounce of my being. I don't care about your past other than it brought you to me. I know God has forgiven you Olivia, and you are pure now; not because of anything you've done, but because of what He's done for you. You're mom is *wrong*. I want you to wear white in our wedding, not because we're trying to hide something, but because that's who you are. You are my bride!"

Olivia calmed down and tried to voice her concerns, but Brad wouldn't hear it. She realized he was right. She thought she had dealt with all of this, but all the doubts and self-condemnation had come roaring back.

"Brad, I know we have to be careful being alone, but will you stay a while? I need to be with you."

"Of course I'll stay. Let's make some popcorn and watch TV. They found an old movie on, Olivia got Joy, and they held her together on their laps. Brad kept his arm around her the whole time, as if to say he'd never let her go. She still felt sad by the end of the evening but knew it was something she had to work through on her own.

Lisa rushed up to Olivia at church the moment she walked in. She wrapped her in a bear hug. "I gave your Mama a piece of my mind after you left, Olivia. I was so mad I couldn't see straight. Gina had to drag me out."

Olivia hugged her back. "Thank you for being such a wonderful friend, Lisa. I love you." She sat between Brad and Lisa during the sermon. Lisa held her hand and Brad had Joy in one arm and his other arm around her. She felt safe and loved, but she knew at some point she'd have to face Mama, and that was bound to be uncomfortable.

At lunch, Brad told Olivia he wanted to go to her Mama and Papa's later that day to talk. "I guess we can Brad, but wouldn't you rather I talked to her? She is going to be angry with me."

"No, Olivia, I want to go alone. I want to protect you from this and let her know where I stand. I don't want her to think she can treat you this way anymore. You're going to be my wife, and I want to take care of you." Olivia couldn't believe he'd do that for her. He was the best thing that had ever happened to her. He asked her to go to Lisa's while he was at Mama and Papa's so he could come back there and talk.

"I wish we could talk at your house, but it's so hard, Olivia. I'll want to hold you, and I know while our emotions are running high we need to be even more careful." Olivia agreed, so Brad dropped her off at Ben and Lisa's.

Lisa tried to distract her while Brad was gone, but Olivia was a mess. Ben suggested they pray. He prayed for Brad to have the right spirit and words, and somehow for Mama to respond well and to understand. It helped having Joy there. She was fun to watch as she was able to crawl around and play with James and Nicole now. Olivia watched her in amazement. This child was a gift, and she realized it was okay if Mama couldn't see that. She and Brad loved each other and loved Joy. God had given them something special, and she was going to be his wife.

A few hours later, they heard Brad's car pull into the driveway. When they saw him, Ben and Lisa took all the kids upstairs so they could talk. He didn't seem defeated when he

Finding Hope

walked in, and Olivia breathed a sigh of relief. "It's going to be fine, Olivia. She understands my wishes."

"What on earth did you say to her?" Olivia asked in disbelief.

"I read her Isaiah 1:18: *Come now, let us reason together, says the LORD. Though your sins are like scarlet, they shall be as white as snow; though they are red as crimson, they shall be like wool.* I explained to her that Christ died for you, and you've been washed as white as snow, and that you're my bride, and I want you to wear white."

Olivia had never had anyone stand up for her at all, let alone to Mama. She couldn't believe Mama had agreed. "I said that I understood it was hard for her, and she didn't have to come along this weekend when you go shopping for dresses if she didn't want to. She decided to let you go with your friends. I hope that's alright." Olivia agreed that it would be best to go with Nora and Lisa.

Lisa made an appointment at another salon because Olivia was too embarrassed to go back to the first one. They agreed on the last Saturday in March.

That evening Olivia and Brad had an appointment with the realtor to view a couple of houses. The first one they saw had one bedroom, and they knew it would be too small for them.

The next house was a white cape cod with a front porch. They walked up the short sidewalk and the realtor let them in. The living room opened to a short hallway. To the right there was a bathroom and two bedrooms. To the left was a doorway to the second level; a long room the length of the house. It could be used as another bedroom once Joy was older. The kitchen wasn't much with an eat-in dining room. There were steps to a basement, and that was where the laundry area was. There was also a room to store canning jars. Olivia had never canned, but Lisa promised to teach her. There was another dingy room in the basement. Brad told her his dad could help them fix it up; maybe turn it into a playroom.

The little yard was surrounded by shrubs and offered privacy from the houses that were so close. Even though it was nothing fancy, Olivia and Brad both liked it. They decided to put an offer on it.

It needed a little "TLC", but both Brad and Olivia were anxious to make it their own. The realtor promised to call as soon as he heard back from the sellers. They decided to go back to Ben and Lisa's so they could wait for the call together.

After a roast chicken dinner, they were playing a game of Euchre when the phone rang. Everyone fell silent and waited while Brad spoke with the realtor. When he hung up, he swung Olivia around. "We got it, Olivia!" They all cheered. Olivia and Lisa couldn't believe they were going to live a few streets apart. They began plans to decorate right away, while Brad and Ben talked about the yard and mortgages.

It was dress-shopping day again, and Olivia felt excited. Lisa and Nora picked her up and they headed to the shop in the next town. When they arrived at the salon, Olivia eyed her friends. "Let's hope this time goes a bit smoother." She walked in and was greeted by a bridal consultant named Claire. As they walked to her desk, Olivia told her what kind of dress she had in mind. The consultant wrote the details down and then motioned them to follow her.

"Okay, Olivia, now for the fun part. Let's go find some dresses." Claire studied her for a moment, "I'm thinking you'll wear a size six. You check out our displays and tell me what you like. I'll run to the back and pull a few that I think fit what you described. Then you'll try them on."

Olivia picked three, and Claire also came back with three. Outside the changing area was a mirror and runway with chairs around it for her friends to sit. Olivia and Claire disappeared into the dressing room to try on the first dress. As she walked out, the girls "oohed and ahhed", and Olivia scrutinized herself in the mirror. It was a beautiful dress, but it wasn't her; same with the second and third. By the fourth dress, she began to feel a little discouraged – maybe she was being too picky. Claire reassured her that sometimes it took several trips, but they'd find the perfect dress for her special day. As Claire buttoned the fifth dress, Olivia wondered if she ought to try a few salons.

She walked out and the girls gasped. "Oh, Olivia, it's beautiful!" Lisa sighed, Nora wiped away tears, and Claire clapped her hands. Olivia walked up to the mirror and was blown away. It was what she'd been dreaming for. Simple and elegant. The top had a sweetheart neckline and stayed tight through her torso, then flared out at the waist. It was satin and had no embellishments, but it was stunning. Olivia felt like a princess.

"I think we've found our dress, ladies!" Claire called in the seamstress who pinned several spots to make alterations. After another hour or so, they were able to head to lunch.

When Olivia got home, she wrapped her arms around Brad and told him again what an amazing man he was. They decided to go out for dinner with Joy so they could talk for a while. Olivia got Joy changed and packed her diaper bag, while Brad waited for them downstairs. When they came down, he took the baby and loaded her in the car. All the way to Flo's, she babbled to herself. Brad and Olivia were content to sit and listen. They chose a booth out of the way so no one would trip over Joy's high chair.

"My parents wanted to know if we could come next weekend. Both of my brothers will be home, and they want to meet you and Joy." Olivia was excited to meet the rest of his family and agreed. They decided to leave on Friday morning so they could have a little more time than the last visit. Olivia was nervous about traveling in the car so long with Joy, but Brad reassured her that she would be fine.

On the trip, she napped for the first hour, and they marveled at what a well-behaved baby she was. They stopped for coffee and a snack. When Brad shut the door, it woke Joy up and she began to cry.

She cried and cried. No matter what Olivia did to try to soothe her, she wouldn't calm down. "She'll cry it out for a few minutes and be fine, Olivia. Don't worry." Four hours later she was still crying, and Brad and Olivia thought they might go crazy. They knew she was okay because when they stopped for a break and took her out of her car seat, she cheered right up. She just wanted to get out and play. The last hour was pure misery, with Olivia's head pounding and Brad a little grumpy. When they pulled up to the Parks' house, they shot out of the car as fast as they could.

Brad unloaded the car, and Joy stopped crying as soon as Olivia lifted her from her car seat. She shook her head in disbelief at how she calmed down once she got what she wanted. Brad's mom threw open the door and ran down the steps to greet them. She saw they were stressed. "Long trip?" Olivia told her how little Joy had cried almost the entire way. "Come on in. I'll get you both some iced tea and ibuprofen."

Mrs. Parks took Joy and carried her upstairs. Olivia could hear her talking to her about all the fun she and grandma were going to have together. Even though she was weary from the temper tantrum, she still felt grateful. Who would've ever thought she and Joy would have a family like this?

Brad carried luggage in and then came downstairs for his ibuprofen. They all sat around the table, and Mrs. Parks served sandwiches and doted on baby Joy. Mr. Parks chuckled when he came in to join them. "Your Mother is in heaven, Brad. She's been waiting to get her hands on that baby. You're lucky you got a sandwich!" They all laughed and saw that it was true. Mrs. Parks was snuggling her and smiling.

"It's my first grandchild, B. G. What did you think I would do? By the way, Brad's brothers won't arrive until tomorrow morning. We figured you'd be tired out tonight from the drive."

Olivia breathed a sigh of relief. After that stressful drive, it would be nice to relax and rest before she met the rest of the family. Mrs. Parks shooed them out of the kitchen after they'd eaten. "Take Olivia for a walk, Brad. B. G. and I will watch the baby."

Brad took Olivia down the path by the river, and they cherished the quiet. Once they reached the water, they took a seat on a tree stump and watched the water go by. After a few minutes, Olivia looked at him. "Are you sure you want to marry me? Traveling to your parents won't be the same."

Finding Hope

He took her hand and confessed, "I admit, I was glad when we got here, but I wouldn't trade a life with you for anything!" Olivia sighed in contentment.

Once Brad's brothers arrived they were busy from sunrise to sunset with the activities Mary had planned for them. They played miniature golf, and Olivia enjoyed seeing a silly side of Brad when he competed with his brothers for eighteen holes. They cheered for Rocky in Rocky II at the Movie Plex downtown and walked to Jumbo Jim's ice cream parlor every evening after dinner.

Brad's brothers, Brandon and Bryce, accepted Olivia and Joy with no questions. Brandon's wife was shy but seemed nice. Olivia marveled at how she had gone from alone in the world to someone with friends and family to spare. As they headed home, she praised God once again for all He'd given her.

Chapter 16

Olivia and Brad began to meet with Pastor Dave each week for pre-marital counseling. One particular session, they discussed the roles that were expected of each of them once they were married. She was thankful Brad wanted her to be a homemaker because this was what she had always wanted. So it was an easy decision.

Not all decisions were so easy, though. Olivia wanted a large family, and Brad thought he wanted two or three children at the most. Olivia tried to tell Pastor Dave that they would figure it out.

"Some of these decisions seem like they don't matter, but once you're married they will become bigger issues. It's smart to let each other know your hopes and find out if there's some insurmountable obstacle before you tie the knot."

Olivia shook her head, she couldn't think of a thing that would cause them trouble.

Pastor Dave chuckled as they left. It was the same with all the couples he counseled. It was hard to understand the pressures they would face once married with a few children. His ultimate goal with pre-marital counseling was to open the door so the couple felt comfortable talking to him later, when the inevitable issues came up in their marriage. He was happy for them, though. He liked Brad and was glad he had found someone special to share his life with.

In May, the church and Brad's family gave Olivia bridal showers. Nonna flew in for the final weeks before the wedding to help with last minute details, and she would also care for Joy while Olivia and Brad honeymooned.

After supper one evening, Olivia heard a knock at the door. She hadn't expected company and had already changed into

Finding Hope

pajamas. She peeked out the window and was baffled to see several of her friends on her doorstep. She flung open her door, and Lisa threw confetti at her. "What are you doing here?" she asked with a giggle. Nora, Hope, and Gina were blowing horns. Miss Elva was behind them grinning, and she had actual clothes on – not a bikini! Mama was next to Miss Elva, and she held a cake. Olivia ushered them in.

"What's going on?" she asked again.

"You'll see," Miss Elva sang out as some of the girls ran back to their cars. Nonna had put on a pot of tea and was pouring lemonade while they found seats. Olivia's eyes grew wide as the girls came back in arms laden with gifts. She had already had her showers and hadn't expected anything else.

"What else could I need?" Olivia wondered aloud. Miss Elva thrust a gift into her hand.

"Open it!" Miss Elva couldn't contain her excitement. Olivia tore off the paper and saw it was a clothing box from Robertson's. She was nervous to see what was inside, considering Mrs. Elva's flair for the dramatic. When she opened the box, a sheer satin robe slid out. Olivia turned a bright shade of red, and all the ladies laughed – even Mama.

"Open this one!" Nora handed her a box. Olivia opened the package and found a beautiful matching bra and underwear set. Lisa gave her a sexy negligee, and so did Sharon and Hope. Nonna gave her a basket of lotions, perfumes, and bubble bath. Mama handed Olivia her package last. In it was the most beautiful nightgown she had ever seen. It was floor length with an empire waist. The top was lace and the gown was satin – and it was white.

Olivia looked up at Mama. "I decided something white would be perfect," she whispered for Olivia alone to hear. Olivia didn't think Mama had ever done something so kind for her. She turned around and wrapped her arms around her.

"Thank you, Mama. It's beautiful." She kissed her cheek and sat back down on the floor.

Lisa and Nonna passed out cake while everyone chatted. It was a fun evening, and Olivia was excited for the time she would get to wear all these beautiful pieces of lingerie.

"I'm surprised at all this," Nora admitted as they cleaned up.

"Surprised at what?" Lisa encouraged her to go on.

"That you are okay with lingerie and did this shower. I guess I thought Christians were pretty uptight about sex."

"Sex is a gift from God, Nora. We believe it's His plan to enjoy it in marriage."

"That's a misconception that a lot of people have then. I admire you all for that," Nora conceded.

After they finished with clean up and her guests were gone, Olivia was unable to sleep. The thought of a physical relationship with Brad both excited and terrified her.

Before Olivia knew it, it was the night before her wedding. Lisa had invited the girls to stay at her house for Olivia's final night as a single woman. Lisa noticed Olivia's nerves and scooted next to her. "What's wrong?" she whispered so no one heard.

"I'm so nervous about tomorrow night, Lisa. I know since I have a baby that people assume I'm experienced, but I was with Jake twice – and that was two years ago! I don't want to disappoint Brad."

"Olivia, this is going to be wonderful for you guys. I know your last experience was difficult. Please don't let your past ruin this beautiful part of marriage." Olivia swiped at the tear falling down her cheek. Nora came to her other side and hugged her, and Hope sat at her feet.

"Nora, would it bother you if we prayed for Olivia as she gets ready to start her life with Brad?" Nora looked unsure, but agreed. They gathered around her and God's peace flooded Olivia's heart once again. She was up late lifting her petition that God would be with her and help her to leave her past behind.

The next morning, the girls got up and started their preparations. Gina did their hair and makeup. They had decided to put their dresses on at church, and soon they were on their way.

When they pulled up to the church, Lisa ran in to make sure Brad was nowhere around. They walked down to their dressing room. On the table was a large bouquet of white roses and a card.

Finding Hope

Olivia picked up the card and read the words from her husband-to-be: "I can't wait to begin our life together, my beautiful bride."

All the girls "oohed and ahhed" over the flowers, and Hope snapped pictures left and right. There was a knock at the door, it was Olivia's Mama. "Can we come in?"

"Of course, Mama! I've been waiting for you to help me into my dress!" So Olivia's Mama and Nonna came in. As Olivia stepped into her dress, Mama zipped her up and adjusted her veil. She told her how beautiful she was, and Olivia was touched by her kindness.

Then Nonna pulled out her bag. "I have a few things for you, Olivia. I bought you a blue garter!" The girls all giggled as Nonna pulled out the garter. It was hideous! It was aqua blue with sequins, feathers, and ribbons. "I wanted you to have something that'd help you smile once you're standing up front. I know how nervous you are and thought this might make you laugh. Plus you needed something blue!" Olivia did laugh as she pulled the garter on. Then Nonna pulled out a beautiful pair of diamond earrings that she had bought herself on their 40th anniversary.

"Oh, Nonna, they're perfect!"

Nonna put them in her ears. "And now you have your 'something old' and 'something borrowed'"! Lisa had been keeping watch and let them know it was time. All the guests were seated, and it was time to walk down the aisle.

When the doors opened and Olivia saw Brad waiting for her at the front of the church, her anxiety melted away. He was so handsome in his tuxedo, and the expression of love in his eyes was more than she felt she deserved. Papa offered his arm and they walked toward the man of her dreams. When they reached the altar, Papa kissed her cheek and gave her hand to Brad.

Through their vows, Olivia was unaware of anyone else. She knew Brad meant every word that came out of his mouth. He was a man of integrity. When Pastor Dave said, "You may now kiss your bride." Brad lifted her veil and kissed her tenderly. She melted into his arms and knew she had nothing to fear on the honeymoon. Pastor Dave introduced them as Mr. and Mrs. Brad Parks. The congregation erupted with claps and cheers.

"Shall we, Mrs. Parks?" Brad grinned as he held out his arm. Olivia took it, willing to walk with him to the ends of the earth.

After greeting all the well-wishers, Brad and Olivia made their way downstairs for the cake and punch reception. They cut the cake and fed each other a piece. They opened gifts while their friends visited. Olivia wasn't sure how all the gifts she received at the shower and the wedding would even fit into their little house. The time flew by, and soon it was time to leave for the honeymoon.

Everyone cheered and tossed rice as they ran to the car. Olivia turned while they pulled away, to see the people who had become her family. Brad reached over to hold her hand. As she clasped his hand, she knew she had a lifetime of happiness to experience with her new husband.

Chapter 17

3 Months later

Lisa had taken Joy for the night so Olivia and Brad could have a romantic evening alone. She splurged on steaks and spent the afternoon digging through boxes to find the perfect dishes. A cake that she had decorated with fresh-cut flowers sat on the counter; like she'd seen in her *Better Homes and Gardens* magazine. She wore Brad's favorite dress and let her hair tumble down her back. She had waited all day for him to come home and sweep her into his arms. Then they would eat by candlelight, while they gazed into each other's eyes and shared their hopes and dreams.

Instead, when Brad arrived home he kissed Olivia's cheek. "Hi, honey, dinner looks great." Before she could respond, he had moved through the kitchen into the living room, and the soft sound of piano music she had playing was replaced by the news on television.

Olivia called Brad to the table and waited for him to compliment her on her dress and express his excitement over an evening alone. "You look nice, Olivia." Brad picked up his knife to cut his steak. She nodded and listened while he talked about work, all the while she wondered what was happening to their romantic night. "After supper you want to eat dessert in the living room? The game is on soon."

"That's fine, Brad, go ahead. I'll clean up." Olivia fumed as she washed dishes. *Maybe he'll figure it out if I serve his dessert and sashay off to bed. Then he'll turn off the tv and we can have some romance tonight.* She cut the beautiful cake she had decorated and set his plate on the coffee table. "Is that all you need, Brad?"

"Thanks, Olivia," he replied, not taking his eyes from the screen.

"Well, I guess I'll go read in my room for a while then." She waited a moment. She wanted to make sure he had a chance to realize how insensitive he had been.

"Okay, enjoy the quiet." And with that she lost him to the game.

Olivia couldn't believe what a turn the night had taken. She fell into a restless sleep and woke when Brad came to bed. When he tried to put his arm around her, she pushed him away. They settled on their sides of the bed and not a word was spoken.

In the morning Olivia waited for an apology, but it never came.

Brad knew she was upset but couldn't figure out why. It had been such a great night, supper was fantastic, and they were able to relax and not worry about Joy's bedtime routine. Then when it was time for bed, Olivia put on the brakes. He received the cold shoulder at breakfast, and now she was in the kitchen. He thought about going in, but decided he'd let her work it out. *She'll open up when she's ready.*

A few hours later, Ben pulled in the driveway with Joy. Brad escaped out the back door to greet him. "Hey, Brad, how was your night?"

"I thought it was great, but Olivia is upset right now. She hasn't talked to me all day."

"What happened?"

"Well, I got home, we ate and then I watched the game while she read in our room. Then –"

"You watched the *game*?" Ben asked with an incredulous glance towards the station wagon where Lisa waited with the kids. "Oh man, you're lucky you're still *alive*. Lisa would've killed me if we had a night alone and I turned sports on instead of talking." Ben chuckled at the confusion on Brad's face.

"She got to read. I thought we were supposed to relax and enjoy a quiet evening. Why didn't she tell me what she wanted?" Ben's chuckle turned into a guffaw, and he slapped Brad on the back.

"You've got a lot to learn, Brad!"

Brad sighed as his friend pulled away. Joy snuggled against his shoulder. *Maybe seeing Joy will pull Olivia out of her funk.*

"Guess who's home?" Brad carried Joy into the house and found Olivia in the kitchen. She reached for Joy in delight.

"How's my sweet girl?" Olivia took Joy to her room, and Brad wondered how she was able to be so distant to him and so loving to Joy at the same time.

While Olivia played with Joy on the floor, her mind wandered to Jake. He had been so romantic and thoughtful. If they had a night alone, he wouldn't have turned the television on. He would have romanced her and noticed all the things she had done to make the evening special. Then she realized she was right. Jake was romantic. He'd had a lot of practice. She didn't want a sweet talker or someone who always took her breath away. She wanted what she had; a hard working man who loved her. A man who was faithful and kind. He may not be as romantic as they come, but he was what she needed.

Olivia knew she had to talk to Brad but was embarrassed at how childish she'd been in using the silent treatment to punish him. When they sat down for supper, Brad prayed, "Dear Lord, thank you for this food, and I thank you for Olivia who prepared it. Please be with us tonight and protect our marriage from the enemy. In Jesus' name, amen." With that Olivia rushed to him.

"I'm so sorry, Brad. I know I should've told you what was wrong. I was so excited for time to spend with you and was crushed when you chose a football game over me. You didn't even notice all the work I did to set the table or that I wore your favorite dress."

"Olivia, I told you everything looked nice and that the food was great. What else did you want me to say?"

Olivia blushed. "I'm being ridiculous. Don't worry about it, okay?"

"No, I do want to know. I thought we'd had a nice time. Well, until you pushed me away later."

"I guess what I wanted was you to take me in your arms, declare your undying love for me, and then talk to me all night."

Olivia giggled as she heard herself speak. It sounded like a little girl's idea of romance. "I guess I ruined our night by having unrealistic expectations."

Brad grinned, "I guess I blew it, too. I should've known football wasn't on your list for our time together. I'm sorry, Olivia. Next time talk to me, though. I'm no good at this stuff. I love you, and I want to work on it." Then Joy dumped her spaghetti over the edge of her high chair, so Olivia grabbed a washcloth to clean it up, and Brad picked up Joy. "I'll wash her up while you do that."

Olivia's heart was light as she chased down all the noodles and wiped sauce from the baseboards and floor. Brad was a wonderful man. She was blessed beyond measure.

Olivia was thrilled to care for her little family. As she set the table for supper, Joy played at her feet. Brad was ready to expand their family. Olivia suspected she was pregnant and had made a doctor's appointment for the following Friday. It was hard to keep it a secret, but she didn't want to get Brad's hopes up until she knew for sure.

Olivia heard Brad's car pull into the driveway, and scooped Joy up to meet him at the door. Brad greeted them with hugs and kisses then took Joy from Olivia. They moved to the kitchen for supper preparations.

"How was your day, Brad?" Olivia glanced up as she set the salt and pepper shakers on the table. He reached up and pulled her into his lap for another kiss instead of an answer. Olivia giggled, "I have to get supper off the stove or it'll burn!" She scurried to the stove and soon served him and Joy their supper. "Lisa called to see if we want to go on a double date next weekend. What do you think?" Olivia asked. They decided to walk over and visit with them after supper and make plans.

While the guys checked out Ben's new lawn mower, Lisa and Olivia took turns pushing the kids in the swing. "I can't believe it's September already. Pretty soon we won't be able to be outside with the kids."

"I think it will be a productive time to get the baby's room ready." Olivia tried to talk in a quiet voice so the guys didn't hear.

"You're pregnant?" Lisa squealed in delight.

"I think so, but I go see Dr. B next week to find out. I haven't told Brad yet. I want to surprise him." Olivia promised to call Lisa as soon as she knew for sure. The sun began to set, and Olivia and Brad left to walk home. Joy babbled in her stroller as they walked and talked. Olivia was happier than she ever dreamed she could be.

Olivia kept busy while Brad worked. She loved taking care of her home. She painted all the rooms and was busy making a quilt for their bed. Her cooking skills had improved, thanks to Lisa and her *Betty Crocker* cookbook. It had pictures and instructions on how to make all kinds of things. Brad always ate what she cooked without complaint. She supposed that anything tasted better than the *Hamburger Helper* that Brad ate almost constantly when he was single.

On Friday morning, Olivia dropped Joy off at Lisa's before going to her doctor's appointment. She waited in an exam room while they processed the results. The nurse came in and confirmed what she had known in her heart. "You're going to have a baby!"

When Brad got home from work, Olivia tried to contain her excitement until he sat down. "I have some exciting news for you and thought we should celebrate."

Brad began to guess at what the news could be. "Your mom called and didn't complain about anything," he joked. Olivia laughed.

"No, that's not it." Brad raised his eyebrows as he waited for her to go on. "We're going to have a baby, Brad!" He jumped up and lifted Olivia in the air.

"We're going to have a baby!" he shouted and swung her around.

That weekend they stopped to visit her Mama and Papa. Olivia tried to chat, but Mama was in a foul mood. Olivia set the table in silence. She longed to have a close relationship with her, but no matter how hard she tried, Mama didn't respond. She resolved to have a different kind of relationship with Joy and any other children God would bless her with.

They stayed a few hours. Papa and Brad played with Joy, and Olivia and Mama talked about things that didn't matter to Olivia.

On the drive home, Olivia and Brad wondered why Mama was so unhappy. They prayed for her to come to know Christ and experience true peace and joy. Olivia didn't want to be negative, but she couldn't picture Mama any other way.

Before they knew it, it was the end of November and time for Olivia's first appointment. They waited in the exam room for Dr. B. When the door swung open, she greeted them in her exuberant manner and plopped down on her trusty stool. "Well, if it isn't my favorite girl and her husband!" Brad reached his hand out, and Doc gave it a hearty shake. Brad stepped aside while Olivia and Doc talked.

"Well, from the test and the dates you gave, you'll be due in the middle of June. I'm going to listen for the heartbeat today." As she squirted the gel on Olivia's belly, Brad watched in wonder of how all this worked. When the room filled with the whooshing sound of the baby's heartbeat, his face lit up.

"That's our baby?" Brad listened in awe.

Doc got a big smile on her face. "It sure is!" She finished her exam and told Olivia she'd see her next month. Olivia couldn't wait to experience a pregnancy with the support of a husband; free of the shame and guilt she had felt when she carried Joy. *No more harsh judgment and discrimination either! Thank you, Lord.*

Lisa and Olivia talked a lot about the baby and how things would change for her and Brad with two children. They started to work on a quilt and spent many afternoons together. Olivia paid a little more attention to the dynamics of a family with two children. She wanted to learn all she could ahead of time to be better prepared. While the children napped, they would sew or try new recipes. Olivia always dreamed of having a sister and felt like she finally had one.

December arrived with the usual parties, family, and food. In addition to working on the baby room, Olivia prepared a room for Brad's parents. They were to arrive the next day, and Olivia was nervous. She wanted them to feel welcome and see that she took good care of Brad and Joy. She was up late as she put the finishing touches on their room. Brad convinced her to come to bed to get some rest. "Olivia, it's fine. They love you already! They're going to be very comfortable."

"I know. I want them to know how happy I am to host them. Do you think they'll be happy about the baby? Or will they think it's too soon?"

Brad laughed in disbelief. "Olivia, you're crazy! My mom has wanted grandchildren for *years*. She's going to be *ecstatic*, and my dad will be happy, too." Olivia knew it would be okay, but she would be glad once the whole family heard the news.

The next afternoon, Brad came home from work so he could be there when his parents arrived. His mom admired their Christmas tree and Olivia's table decorations. She rolled up her sleeves and helped get supper ready while they waited for Mama and Papa to join them.

Soon there was a knock on the door. Brad welcomed his in-laws and said, "Just in time. Supper's almost ready!" Brad's dad and Papa raved over the spaghetti and garlic toast, but Mama wasn't one to give a kind word. "She makes her own sauce. I'm so proud of how she makes meals special." After supper Brad cleared his throat. "We wanted to have all of you over together because we have some exciting news." They turned to him in expectancy. "Olivia and I found out we're going to have a baby!"

Mary jumped up and gave hugs all around. She began to ask questions, and Olivia couldn't help but laugh. B. G. and Papa congratulated them, and at last Mama did as well. It was obvious she didn't approve, though. She thought it was too soon for another baby, and that put a damper on the festivities. Olivia felt sad that no matter what she did, she couldn't seem to connect with Mama

The next day, Brad and his dad drove to the ski resort, while Olivia and Mary spent the day in the kitchen. They prepared a chicken pot pie, homemade applesauce, and a tossed salad. Then they sipped on tea and chatted about the coming changes to their family. There was a lull and both were quiet for a few minutes.

"You know, Olivia, I don't want to pressure you. But B. G. and I would be thrilled if you'd call us mom and dad."

"I would be honored." Both women grew teary. Olivia knew she was truly loved by Brad's parents.

When she and Brad lay in bed that night, she told him how much it meant to her to be loved by his family.

"I want our family to be like yours was when you were growing up, Brad. I want a house full of children and to be fun and joyful." Brad stroked her hair and told her he wanted the same thing. Thoughts of laughter and children danced in Olivia's head as she drifted off to sleep.

Chapter 18

January 1981

After Christmas, Olivia and Lisa were on their way home from Bible study when Lisa mentioned she was pregnant, too.

"What?" Olivia couldn't believe it. "Are you serious?"

Lisa laughed. "I am! I found out yesterday! I'm due in August!" They spent the afternoon planning their children's lives. They decided Olivia would have a boy and Lisa would have a girl. Someday they'd get married and they'd all be family.

Brad and Ben laughed as their wives planned for the babies' future over the coming months. For once, Olivia didn't fear for her future. She knew Brad would be there and that their children would have a godly man for their father. She loved each moment of her pregnancy. At night, she and Brad would lay in bed and feel the baby kick. He would tell her about work, and she would share about her and Joy's time at home.

In the spring, Olivia and Brad often took long walks, and they began to discuss baby names. They decided on the name Bradley David for a boy, but they'd call him David. They settled on Sarah Elizabeth if it was a girl.

Brad wouldn't let her paint the nursery or set up any furniture. He did it all himself. One evening in May, Olivia sat on the floor folding clothes when she felt another contraction. Dr. B had told her not to worry about the contractions she was having; and that Braxton-hicks occur more frequently with each subsequent pregnancy. Still, it made her feel unsettled. She wasn't due for three more weeks, yet they were getting stronger. She tried to get up off the floor, but needed a helping hand. "Brad, could you come in here and help me up?"

Brad walked into the living room and had to smile. "What would you have done if I wasn't home?"

Olivia didn't want to be teased. She was the size of a whale and hadn't felt good all day. "Oh, I don't know. Maybe I would have had Joy finish the laundry and I would just lay down here and go to sleep!"

"I'm sorry, Olivia. I don't mean to tease. I know it's getting hard." Brad helped her up and asked if she needed a back rub.

"That would be great. I just need to put these clothes away and check on Joy first." When she bent over to pick up the clothes, her water broke. She stared at the floor in disbelief.

"What's the matter, Olivia?"

"I think my water broke. I don't know if that's normal because I have three more weeks to go. We need to find someone to watch Joy and head to the hospital."

Brad just stared at her.

"Brad, can you call Lisa?" She asked again. He nodded his head, and Olivia rushed off to change and pack her bag. By the time Lisa arrived, she had begun having regular contractions. They prayed together and Olivia promised to call her as soon as the baby was born. She kissed Joy goodbye. The next time she saw her, she'd be a big sister!

They got in the car and Brad drove like an old man. He was afraid to cause Olivia any more discomfort. At the hospital, Dr. B bustled in to check her. She determined it would still be a few hours. Olivia was at five centimeters. "Is it okay to have the baby before my due date?" Olivia asked with some concern.

"Oh, sure honey. We wouldn't want to be much earlier, but babies born at thirty-seven weeks are fine." Olivia breathed a sigh of relief. Brad stayed by her side and stroked her arm to soothe her when a contraction came. As the hours passed and the pain became more intense, Olivia thought back to when Joy was born. She was grateful that Lisa and Hope were by her side then, but it was so different to have Brad. His strength was a comfort to her. She knew the time was getting close and she was beginning to have the urge to push. The nurse called Dr. B in to check her again.

"Looks good! You can go ahead and push with the contractions now!"

Olivia's heart raced. *Soon our baby will be here!* She bore down with everything she had. In between pushes, Brad kept telling her she was doing great. Dr. B was coaching her too. "Looks like the next one will do it. Now push! Push! Push!"

Olivia bore down hard. "That's it!" said Dr. B. The baby's head emerged. She glanced at Brad in jubilation.

Dr. B said, "Oh, I am so sorry. There's a problem with the mouth. Olivia, you have to push again, let's get these shoulders out." Olivia continued to push hard, and soon a baby boy entered the world. Dr. B began to bark out orders for the nurse to get the pediatrician and call NICU at Elmwood. Several nurses entered the delivery room and began working on Bradley David.

Doc continued to stitch up Olivia. Brad hung on tightly to Olivia's hand and they looked at each other in fear. Bradley David was whisked away. When Dr. B was finished, she pulled her stool next to Olivia and took her hand. She motioned for Brad to have a seat. They both stared in disbelief as they waited for Doc to speak.

"You have a baby boy, but he has a cleft lip and palate. There are surgeries that can fix that, but he needs to be evaluated right away to make sure there are no other problems. We're calling Elmwood Baptist Hospital to transfer him because we don't have a Neonatal Intensive Care Unit here at this hospital. We are going to hope for the best, but we want to be thorough."

"Can I see him?" Olivia said, still in shock.

"We have to put him in an Isolette, Olivia. You won't be able to hold him, but we will wheel him in before they transport him." Olivia couldn't find words for her emotions. She nodded her head in agreement. Dr. B left the room. Brad sat staring into space. Neither knew what to say or do.

Olivia was transported back to her room. She and Brad wondered when they would get to see little Bradley David. When the pediatrician came to her room, the news was worse than they ever could have imagined. They had a special transport unit coming to get him. Olivia tried to get up. "No Olivia," Dr. Batten ordered. "I'm so sorry, but you aren't ready to be released yet.

They have no open beds in the obstetric unit at Elmwood Baptist, so we need to keep you here a few more days. You lost a lot of blood."

"Go with him, Brad," Olivia begged. "Please don't leave him." Brad was almost paralyzed with shock. "Go!" Olivia shouted.

When he left, she collapsed on the bed in hopes that this was a nightmare and would wake up soon. Her arms were empty and so were her dreams of a happy future. There was a soft knock at the door. Olivia watched as it opened. It was Lisa. She was due any day and Olivia couldn't bear to see her. They sat in silence. After a while, Lisa began to talk, "Can I do anything, Olivia? Can I make phone calls, bring clothes, please tell me what to do." Olivia gave her a list of phone numbers and told her she wanted to be alone.

Brad's parents flew in that night. Mary rushed to Olivia and hugged her. "B. G. is with Brad, and I'm staying with you." Olivia asked her to keep people out. She couldn't handle visitors. In the morning, Olivia's own parents had yet to call. She asked Mary if they had been told. Olivia watched as she struggled with what to say, and knew. They knew. This was more than Mama could deal with. She would pretend it hadn't happened.

The weeks passed in a blur. Olivia tried to split her time between David at the hospital and Joy at home. Joy was too young to spend long days in the NICU. Olivia spent hours rocking her little boy and praying. Brad came up when he could, but he had to work. Most of the time Olivia was alone. Mama and Papa hadn't come up at all, and Nora just once. Thankfully Nonna had flown up the minute she found out and was taking care of Joy while Olivia was at the hospital.

Tests revealed that David had a hole in his heart as well as a bilateral cleft lip and palate. He also had a club foot and was missing his corpus callosum, the bundle of neural tissue that connects the left and right sides of the brain. The prognosis wasn't good. He was on a feeding tube, so Olivia was unable to even feed her son. A tear slipped down her cheek as she studied his face. As much as she wanted support when someone did come up, she felt

Finding Hope

nervous. She didn't want anyone gawking at David. Lisa wasn't able to come up at all. She was due any day, and it was too far of a drive to chance it. Olivia was relieved. Being around a pregnant woman would be difficult right now. The pain was too raw.

A choking sound broke her out of her thoughts. As the alarms sounded, the nurse rushed towards David. She watched her son in desperation. They were able to suction him, but after that he had to go back to the Isolette. Nurse LuAnn spoke up. "Olivia, why don't you call it a day. You've been here ten hours. You know I'll care for him like he's mine. Go snuggle that little girl of yours." Olivia hadn't noticed the time. She packed up, stroked David's cheek, and drove home.

"Mama, Mama," Joy shouted as Olivia picked her up when she got home. She gave her a kiss and found Nonna cooking supper. Olivia sank into the chair by the table and set Joy down. "Play Mama?" Joy asked, hopeful that tonight she could spend time with her Mama.

"Not tonight baby. Mama is tired." Joy ran off to the living room.

Not long after, Brad came in looking hopeful. "Any change?" Olivia shook her head. Sometimes words were too much. He gave her a hug, and walked to the living room and found Joy. She could hear them playing and wished she could join them, but her legs wouldn't move to take her there.

Each day was the same: hours at the hospital alone, time at home helping Nonna with household chores, then to bed. The routine and stress had worn her down. One day in the NICU, a nurse came and told her that she had a phone call. It was Nonna. "Olivia, you need to come home. Joy has been crying for you all morning. I couldn't get her to calm down. Now she's throwing up. She needs you, too, honey."

Olivia felt torn. Both of her children needed her. How could she leave David when he was struggling for each breath. What if he died while she was gone? But her little girl needed her, too. Once again she felt like a failure. She packed her things and let

Nurse LuAnn know she was leaving. Nurse LuAnn took one look at her and gave her a big hug.

"How do people do this, LuAnn? It's been a month, and I'm exhausted. I feel guilty if I leave Joy, and I feel guilty if I leave David." How long will this last?" LuAnn rubbed her back and tried to comfort her.

"Olivia, I wish I had answers. I don't know how this will all work out, but it will. This won't go on forever."

As Olivia drove home she cried out to God, but it seemed to fall on deaf ears. When she got home Joy was a mess, Nonna was frazzled and worried. "I'm sorry I had to call you, Tesoro, but I can't calm her down."

Joy ran with arms stretched out for her. "I'll give her a bath, Nonna. You go rest." Olivia bathed Joy and then rocked her until she fell asleep. She lay her down in bed next to her and fell into a troubled sleep herself.

Brad felt helpless. He didn't know how to comfort his wife, he didn't know how to help his son, and he didn't know how to make sense of any of it. It was so hard to go into a room of students each day and teach. It took *all* of his energy. Then when he got home, Joy was in desperate need of attention. Nonna took wonderful care of her, but Joy missed her mom and dad. Olivia ran herself ragged with long days at the hospital and evenings helping Nonna get caught up at home.

Brad started to take lunch in his classroom, instead of the teacher's lounge, to think and pray. It began to overwhelm him to sit with the others. Conversation was often stilted around him because his friends weren't sure what to say. It wasn't that they didn't care. They were afraid to cause more pain. He wished they could see that no words were necessary, and that his Christian friends didn't need to try and explain God's ways. He knew that God is good – and believed it. What he *wanted* was a friend to walk through this tragedy with him; to listen if he needed an ear or to grieve with him.

Finding Hope

Brad heard a light knock on his classroom door a few minutes before class was to resume. He glanced up to see Ben. "Hey man, can I come in?"

"Sure." Brad was surprised to see him. Ben had taken the last week off to help Lisa with the kids before the baby was born. "Did Lisa get sick of you?" Brad tried to joke, but the words seemed to fall flat.

Ben pulled a chair up beside him. He was nervous. "I wanted to stop by and tell you myself. Lisa had the baby this morning. It was a girl." He looked down at his hands. "I'm so sorry, Brad. I don't know what to say." For the first time since Brad had known him, Ben began to cry.

"Thanks for telling me, Ben. Is she –" Brad struggled to get the words out. "Is she healthy?" Ben nodded. "It's okay Ben, I'm happy for you guys."

"I know, but it's so hard, Lisa misses Olivia. She wasn't sure if she should call her to let her know. I'll leave that up to you."

Brad sighed. "I think I'll tell her. I don't know how much she can handle right now. I think a hospital visit would be too much on her. You know we love you guys. Give her some time." They shook hands, and Ben left to go back and be with Lisa. Brad's heart sank. *How am I going to tell Olivia? How much more can she take?*

Olivia awoke to find Brad at the side of their bed, looking grim. "What's wrong? Did the hospital call while I was asleep? I knew I shouldn't have left!"

"No, Olivia, nothing like that. Ben stopped by to see me during my lunch hour." Olivia sat up and he continued. "Lisa had the baby last night. It's a girl."

"Is she healthy?"

"She's fine." They stared at each other. There were no words to express the sorrow of what could have been. A boy and a girl. This was what she and Lisa had *dreamed* of. They could've nursed the babies, rocked them, and marveled over them together. Instead, Lisa was celebrating and Olivia was suffering. Where was God in this? After she had done things the right way, why had this happened? Brad held her while she cried.

The following month, Olivia was at the hospital when Dr. Jensen came in. He finished his morning rounds and stopped at David's Isolette to schedule a meeting with her and Brad as soon as they could. He wanted to discuss the course of treatment. Olivia knew it was hopeless. They'd already determined he wouldn't improve unless a miracle took place. She called Brad at work, and they decided to meet that evening in the hospital cafeteria to talk. Next Olivia called Nonna to let her know she'd be late coming home.

At 5:00 p.m., Olivia left David and headed down to get a table. Brad slid in next to her moments later and held her hand. Once upon a time that thrilled her, but now she couldn't feel a thing. Dr. Jensen shook hands with Brad and sat down. They looked at him, hopeful for some good news.

With compassion in his voice, the doctor said, "David is not going to get better. He's been here three months, but there's nothing further we can do. I don't want to rush you. Soon, though, you need to decide if you want to take him home–" he hesitated. "Or if you want to put him into a long-term care facility. David will need twenty-four hour care."

Olivia looked at him in horror. This *couldn't* be happening. Was there no hope for her baby boy? "Are there even any facilities like that around here for children?" Brad asked, accepting the doctor's words.

"There are three within a 100-mile radius. They're all quite a drive. I'm sorry there's nowhere closer."

"How do we know which one is best?" Olivia asked.

"Well, I would go visit each place. Meet the staff, take the tour, and take a few weeks to make your decision." Olivia got the phone numbers, and they headed off to see David one more time before they left.

For the next few days, Olivia had to stay home and make phone calls. She set up appointments for tours of each facility.

Finding Hope

They decided to take Joy with them because Nonna was exhausted and Olivia knew she needed some time to rest. Lisa had offered to help with her any time, but Olivia couldn't bear to go over and see the new baby. Besides, it was difficult to be separated from Joy right now; they needed each other.

On a dreary Tuesday morning, they packed the car and headed to the first facility. As the rain poured down, Olivia couldn't help but think that God was weeping. They didn't talk much, but Joy chatted in the back seat to her stuffed bear. Time flew by for Joy but dragged painfully slow for her parents. They finally pulled into the parking lot of Merrifield Manor. Brad turned off the car and reached for Olivia's hand. "Lets pray. We need God's guidance to know what to do – and he may heal David yet. We need to have faith."

Olivia let him pray, but it felt hollow to her. *Faith? My faith has been shattered to pieces.*

As soon as they walked in the door, the fumes hit them. It wasn't dirty, but the stench of urine was in the air. The volunteer greeted them and explained all the things the facility had to offer. As they walked down hall after hall, Olivia grew more and more distressed. All these children shut behind gates and doors. They sat with toys in front of them, but didn't play. Many drooled, and all were in diapers or had catheters. No one smiled. It was a sad place, despite the bright murals painted on the walls. It was a place without hope.

By the time they walked out, Olivia knew she didn't want to see the other homes. Her baby was staying with her – no matter how hard it was. Somehow she would find the help she needed.

When she got home, Olivia called the hospital and told Dr. Jensen her decision. They set up another meeting to discuss the details of caring for David at home. When Olivia hung up, she wandered into the nursery that she had prepared, full of hopes for her child, and cried. She knew it wouldn't be enjoyed the way she'd dreamed of. Instead, it would turn into a critical care room, and it likely would be the room David would die in. She offered up a prayer begging God to heal her son. She knew it was improbable that she'd receive the answer she was desperate for.

Nurse LuAnn taught her how to clean the feeding tube and how to suction the baby when he choked. He was smiling now, as Olivia held him, and she thought it so strange. *How can he smile and coo, and yet be so sick?* To her it was a beautiful smile, but the cleft in his lip was large.

Joy tried to figure it out as best she could. "Ouchie?" she asked as she pointed to his face. Nurse LuAnn tried to explain, but Joy couldn't grasp the situation. That was a blessing because she loved the baby and didn't seem to mind his different appearance.

As Dr. Jensen and LuAnn taught Olivia about David's care over the next days, she grew more and more nervous about the day that she would bring him home. Could she do this? Someone had to be with him around the clock at the hospital. Since Nonna was not up to caring for him and Joy, they had to hire a home nurse to do nights.

Brad was working long hours to try to make ends meet. He took an additional job delivering pizzas two nights a week. Hospital bills flooded their mailbox, and now they'd be adding homecare and medical supplies. Olivia wondered again how they would manage.

Chapter 19

The day arrived for David to come home. Olivia and Brad drove to the hospital to pick him up. They both were terrified of what the next months held. They walked from the parking garage to the NICU in silence. The sound of their footsteps echoed in the empty corridor. Dr. Jensen greeted them inside the unit, and he directed the nurses to unhook David from all the monitors. Brad and Olivia were not taking their son home with the hopes of years spent together. They were taking him home to die.

Upon arriving home, Olivia lifted David out of his car seat and held him in her arms – the first time she'd held him without wires everywhere. She looked down at him with eyes blurred, pleading with God to help her boy.

Brad cleared his throat. "Olivia, I'm here, but I don't know how to help you. Please let me know what to do." Olivia didn't know what he wanted her to say because there was nothing he could do. He walked away heartbroken. He couldn't seem to reach his wife. Nonna kept Joy in the playroom while they began to set up

Nurse Amy arrived at ten o'clock that night to relieve Olivia. She felt a great relief, knowing that David would be well-cared for. Brad was still awake when she slid into bed. He reached for her, but she rolled onto her side and fell into an exhausted sleep. She awoke at six to start her shift. David had a rough night but was doing a little better now. Olivia prepared formula for the feeding tube while Nonna fed Joy. They sat at the table as a family for the first time in weeks. Joy blew kisses to David and he gurgled in response. Nonna tried to be cheerful, but it was so hard to keep up pretenses in the midst of such a devastating set of circumstances. Brad had to leave for work, and they held hands and prayed for God to somehow intervene.

Life revolved around David and his extensive needs in a nerve-wracking routine. On a beautiful day in October, Olivia sat on the porch near her living room window while Joy and David slept. Nonna was knitting in David's room so that Olivia could take a quick break. She heard Nonna shout for her and raced back into the house. David was blue. Olivia suctioned him and he returned to steady breathing.

Olivia was exhausted and felt she couldn't go on much longer. She took David to her room, laid next to him on the bed, and cried out to God: "Please, Lord Jesus, *please* do something. Have mercy on us. Heal him or take him home to be with you." She stroked his head and when she opened her eyes, he seemed to be studying her. She wondered what he was thinking – if anything. Even though the doctors said he'd never walk, or talk, or even know who his mother was, Olivia knew the truth. David smiled whenever she walked in the room. When he had trouble sleeping, Nurse Amy would ask Olivia to hold him for a little bit. He would always fall asleep when he was in her arms.

David's health regressed in the next couple weeks. Olivia didn't want to leave him for very long, for fear that he would pass away without her there. One day his fever reached 105 degrees, and he slipped into a coma. Olivia tried to make him as comfortable as possible, knowing it wouldn't be long.

Nurse Amy came for her normal shift, but Olivia wanted to spend more time with David. She told Amy to help herself to a cup of tea while she rocked her son. After several hours, she was no longer able to keep her eyes open and reluctantly handed David over to the nurse.

That night Olivia didn't sleep well, she got up to use the restroom and peeked in on David. Nurse Amy was standing in the middle of the nursery with David in her arms. Their eyes met and Olivia knew. "He's gone?" The nurse nodded her head and handed him to Olivia. She pulled him close and closed her eyes. He was no longer hot to the touch; his suffering was over.

She felt a hand on her leg and looked down. Joy was awake and stood next to her, pointing at the ceiling. "Pretty, Mama."

Olivia wondered what she could be seeing. She asked the nurse to take Joy to Nonna as she stumbled to her room to get Brad. They grieved together once again over their precious boy. God had answered, but it wasn't the answer they'd longed for.

The next afternoon was pure misery. Olivia had been up all night, and now it was time to go to the funeral home. The funeral director met with them and helped them choose a casket. Olivia didn't know they made them so small. She ached for her son, but he wasn't there to hold. She and Brad made the arrangements: day and time of the funeral, place of the service, and the cemetery where David would be laid to rest.

When they got home, people were already bringing food over. Olivia wanted to scream. Did they think a casserole was going to help her cope with the death of her son? "I'm going to our room and don't want to see anyone."

Hundreds of people attended the funeral, but Olivia was oblivious. What did it matter? She made it through but felt nothing. When Brad tried to comfort her that evening, she was inconsolable. The doorbell rang a few hours later, and Olivia disappeared to her room. She heard some low voices and then Brad knocked on the door.

"Olivia, Dr. B is here. She wants to see you." Olivia didn't respond, but they came in the room anyway.

Dr. B hugged her tight. "Olivia, I am so sorry about this tragedy. I know there is no way I can help you deal with the pain. Brad is worried about you, though, because you need to get some rest. Fatigue compounds the struggle to cope. I have a prescription for you to aid your sleep. I also have information on a grief support group that begins in a few weeks. You can't walk through this alone." Olivia was expressionless as she stared at her. "Do you understand, Olivia?" Dr. B asked. Olivia nodded her head. Brad got a glass of water, and she took a pill that night. It worked. She slept the whole night through for the first time in months.

She awoke the next morning with the thought to check on David. As she opened the door, it hit her fresh that he wasn't there.

Elizabeth Diaz

She stood in the doorway of his nursery, grief-stricken yet again. That was how Nonna found her. "Olivia, I haven't experienced the loss of a child, and I don't pretend to know what you're feeling. But, honey, the way to heal is to take one step at a time. Why don't you take Joy for a walk?" Joy was delighted since she hadn't had much "Mommy time" lately. Olivia put Joy's coat and hat on and they headed to the garage for the stroller.

Nonna began to worry. Olivia had wandered the neighborhood for hours. With Joy asleep in her stroller, she had lost all track of time.

Nonna was cooking when they arrived home. Olivia carried Joy to her bed and kissed her little forehead before she tiptoed out. She reached for her apron and began to help prepare supper. Many weeks passed in the same manner; Nonna mothering Olivia and Joy.

After about six weeks, Nonna told her she needed to go home. "I know you have a lot of grieving left to do, Olivia, but I don't want to get in the way of you caring for Joy. I think taking the responsibilities of the house back over will help you. Brad and Olivia agreed, and Nonna left after Thanksgiving.

Olivia knew she had to somehow get up every morning and be the mom that Joy needed. She didn't want her to grow up without a brother *and* without her mom. Each day she forced herself to shower, get dressed, and make breakfast. Sometimes it was all she could do to lift her arms to rinse the shampoo out of her hair. Olivia was relieved that Joy seemed content with what little she was able to give.

Brad took her to the weekly grief support group. Sometimes it helped, but many times she didn't hear what was discussed because she was so lost in her grief. At one session, the counselor spoke about a way to start the journey back to "normal": help someone else. "Find someone in need and take them a meal, visit a sick friend, or volunteer somewhere." That struck Olivia, and she decided to reach out and help someone once a week.

The first few times, it was more out of desperation than concern for others. But as the weeks progressed, Olivia had some

Finding Hope

moments where she thought of something besides the loss that encompassed her.

Chapter 20

In the spring, six months after David had died, Brad asked Olivia if she wanted more children. She was terrified to face the possibility of another loss. She was angry that he brought it up – and angry that it made her angry. She knew it wasn't unreasonable to try again, but she wasn't ready. She needed to talk but had distanced herself from her friends. She didn't know how to enter back into life.

Olivia decided to go see Pastor Dave while Brad was at work. He led her into his office and offered her a chair. "How are you Olivia? You've been in my thoughts often."

Olivia took a few moments to find the right words. "I'm angry." Pastor Dave didn't seem at all bothered by her confession. "I'm angry at Brad. I'm angry at God. I'm angry with myself. Did I do something to bring this on? Is God punishing me for my past?" She looked at him in confusion. "I don't understand why this happened."

Pastor leaned back in his chair as he gathered his thoughts. "Why are you angry with Brad?"

"He doesn't even seem to care that David is gone. He goes to work, comes home, plays with Joy and that's it. He doesn't ever talk about him. Last week, he asked if I want another baby; like we could go on with life and forget this ever happened."

"People grieve in a different ways, Olivia. Even if Brad doesn't talk with you about it, he's suffering too. The loss of a child is one of the biggest causes of divorce. It's the hardest thing any couple can face. I know it's difficult when you feel alone, but you're not. I've known your husband for quite a few years now, and this has changed him. He is grieving, too."

"I don't know how to talk to him anymore. I don't know if I *want* to."

"Olivia, we can't explain why this happened. It's definitely not your fault. If God took the children of all the people who ever made a mistake, there would be no children."

Olivia sat in silence for several minutes. "I don't know what to do. I feel lost."

Pastor gazed at her with compassion. "There's nothing you can do to lessen the pain. Time will help. My best advice would be to remember that Brad is grieving, also. He's internalizing it more. You both need time, and you can come here anytime to talk." He prayed for them and their marriage before she left.

Olivia thought about her conversation with Pastor Dave often. She knew she was wrong to assume Brad had forgotten David or that he didn't care. She wanted to close the chasm that seemed to separate them but was unsure of what steps to take.

One morning, warmer temperatures and a quiet breeze beckoned Olivia outside. She decided to take Joy for a walk and enjoy the spring morning. She ended up in front of Lisa's house and quickly turned around. She heard the door open and, glancing back, met Lisa's questioning eyes. They both stood still for a moment and then Lisa ran to her. Tears were shed as they clung to each other. No words were necessary.

Lisa invited Olivia in for tea, and she noticed right away that Lisa had repainted the kitchen. She couldn't help but wonder what other changes had happened in her friends' lives during the past year. She sat down while Lisa made the tea. "I'm sorry it's been so long, Lisa. I know things are different, but I want to try to join life again. I really miss you." She waited in anticipation for Lisa's response. It was quiet for a moment.

"I haven't known what to do, Olivia. I am grieving with you. I didn't want to push because I knew how hard would be for you to see Lindsey. I'm sorry if I stayed away too long." They both cried, relieved that they had reconnected and could talk again. The sound of a baby's cry filled the air. Olivia's heart began to pound, and Lisa stood up so fast her chair toppled over. "Lindsey is up. I need to go get her. Do you want to stay a little longer?"

Olivia shook her head. "I'm not ready," she whispered. "I need to go." She bundled Joy up in a hurry and promised to visit again soon. She breathed a sigh of relief when they were outside again. If the sound of Lisa's baby affected her that much, she may never be able to go back to church – or go *anywhere*. It seemed that wherever she turned there was something that reminded her of David.

That night at supper, Brad reached over and held her hand. "The funeral home called today. David's headstone is in. Do you want to go see it?" Olivia nodded her head. Brad called Hope to come stay with Joy while they were at the cemetery. Before now, Olivia would've been skeptical if someone told her a cemetery could bring comfort to her, but it did. It was a way to be near David and a quiet place to grieve.

The headstone read: "Bradley David Parks. April 21, 1981 – September 25, 1981. To God Be the Glory". They stood by the grave a long time. Olivia glanced up at Brad, the first time she had really looked at him since David had been born eleven months ago. She saw how he'd aged, his face etched with grief. She reached for him and he pulled her close. They embraced for a long time. "I'm so sorry, Brad. I know I've been oblivious to your needs. I'm so sorry."

Brad stroked her hair and put his hands on her face. "It's okay, Olivia. I've missed you, but I didn't know what to do. Sometimes when we grieve, we don't see anything but our own pain." They prayed that God would protect their marriage and restore the intimacy they had lost.

That night as they prepared for bed, Olivia knew it was time to be available to her husband's physical needs: to open up her heart again to Brad. When she walked in the room and shut the door, she determined in her heart to begin restoring their marriage in a tangible way.

Spring soon turned to summer. The changing seasons were a constant reminder to Olivia that time marches on, even though her world had fallen apart. Olivia pushed Joy in their backyard swing while Brad grilled. They had invited Ben and Lisa and the kids for

Finding Hope

dinner. Olivia still struggled being around Lindsey, but knew the way to heal was to face those difficult situations. Some times were excruciating, but other times felt normal.

That night, as Lisa was preparing the kid's dinner plates, Lindsey started to cry. Without thinking, Olivia picked her up to comfort her. She held her close and imagined what size David would be if he were here. Lisa sat down next to her, unsure of what to say. A tear found a way down her cheek, but Olivia knew in her heart that it was okay.

When Brad saw her with the baby, he made his way across the yard to her. Ben joined them, and Olivia asked them to pray for her. "Can you pray that I could get back to the routine of life without falling apart every time something reminds me of David?" They had a sweet time together. Olivia was so thankful for the way her friends had reached out and held her up.

As the months passed, Olivia knew it was time to go back to church. At first she sat in the back row. It took time for her to reclaim her spot next to Brad up front. He was the worship leader and had to sit close to the platform. It was still painful to see moms with babies, but she continued to make progress.

One Sunday, she overheard Gina and Lisa talking in whispers in the hallway. She didn't mean to eavesdrop, but she heard Gina tell Lisa she was expecting. Lisa congratulated her, and that was all Olivia heard. The tears came fast, and she hurried to find Brad to take her home.

"I overheard Gina telling Lisa that she was pregnant. I was just around the corner in the hallway. I know it's a normal part of life, but I had to leave." Brad knew the pain was not only from the loss of David but also from the loss of a dream. Olivia was devastated. He didn't know what to say, so he drove her to her favorite place: The Riverwalk. He let her sit by the water while he played with Joy. After a while, she composed herself and walked over to them. "I'm so sorry, Brad. I feel like I'll never be able to handle anything. I am an emotional basket case. I don't want Gina to feel like she can't talk about her pregnancy. How will I *ever* conquer this?"

"It's going to take time, Olivia. It hasn't even been a year since David was born, and it may take *years*. For both of us. Maybe our pregnancy is just around the corner, like Lisa and Gina were." Olivia nodded in agreement. They walked to the car with each of them holding one of Joy's hands.

The next evening, she called Gina to offer congratulations on her pregnancy. It wasn't as difficult as she thought it would be, and Gina was ecstatic. Olivia hadn't known, but she and Chuck had been trying for two years to have a baby. Olivia was happy for them, and *that* was a miracle.

Joy turned three years old over the summer, and Olivia enrolled her in preschool. On the first school morning in September, all Joy could talk about in the car was how much fun it would be. Olivia walked her in and they found the classroom. The building was cheerful and the teachers attentive. She knew it would be beneficial for Joy to have other children to play with. She stayed in the class and chatted a few minutes with the other moms.

On her way home, she decided to stop and see Mama. Mama seemed pleased when she opened the door and saw Olivia. "I was wondering if you were up for company." Mama opened the door wider, and Olivia joined her inside. "I dropped Joy off at preschool and am feeling kind of sad."

"I remember your first day at school. I cried all the way home after I dropped you off."

Olivia smiled. She didn't realize Mama was so sentimental. They played Yahtzee while they visited, and then it was time for Olivia to go pick up Joy.

Joy was excited when Olivia arrived to pick her up. She wanted to show her what she had done. Olivia admired her finger painting and built a tower of blocks with her. She picked her up and carried her to the car. Her baby was growing up.

At supper, Brad and Olivia were talking when Joy spoke up. "I shouldn't have done it." They both turned toward her with eyebrows raised. You never knew what was going to come out of her mouth. Sometimes it was funny and sometimes it was exasperating.

"Shouldn't have done what, sweetie?" Olivia asked nervously.

"I shouldn't have taken it." Brad stifled a chuckle and waited for Joy to go on. "I took a little people from school," she whispered.

"Where did you put it?" Brad asked, wondering if she had taken something or had made it up. Joy slid down from her chair and ran to her book bag. When she returned to the table, she had a Fisher-Price little toy person in her hand.

Olivia peeked over at Brad and tried to hide her grin. "Joy, that's stealing when you take something that doesn't belong to you. "

A little tear ran down Joy's cheek, and Brad lifted her to his lap. He talked about what the Bible had to say about stealing and gave her a kiss. "Put it in your bag, sweetie. You have to give it back." Joy nodded her head and shuffled back to her bag. "It's better than the time she stole the hose nozzle from Pastor Dave!" Brad whispered in Olivia's ear. She giggled, remembering how embarrassed she had been when that happened. Life wasn't dull with Joy around.

Chapter 21

Olivia dreaded the one-year anniversary of David's death. She thought she should have made more progress by now, but most days she broke down at some point. She decided to spend the morning at the cemetery because it was so tranquil. Joy loved going. There was a watering station close to his grave with a bucket. Big sister loved watering the mums around his headstone. She watered wherever she saw a wilting plant, which gave Olivia time to grieve.

"Mommy, remember the pretty angels that took David in the sky?" Joy asked.

Olivia was startled. "What do you mean, Joy?"

"I remember the night he went away. I saw Nurse Amy holding him and there were angels up high. Didn't you see it, Mommy?"

Olivia thought back to that night. She remembered Joy coming into the room when David had died and pointing at the ceiling. *Could it be? Had she seen angels?* The thought gave Olivia much-needed comfort. She held her close for a minute before Joy was off to water more plants. She eventually packed up their things and helped Joy into the car. Joy talked nonstop during the ride home. *Thank you, Lord. This little girl has kept me from drowning in my grief.*

That evening, Brad brought home some flowers with a simple card. He had written on the back of the card: "I'll never forget." It was a sad day, but she was thankful for the time spent in quiet at the cemetery.

The phone rang a few days later, and Olivia hustled to answer. "Hello?"

"Hi, Olivia, it's Nonna. Guess what?" Nonna always lifted her spirits. They had spent hours on the phone since David had passed. She didn't know what she would have done without her.

"What Nonna? I won't even pretend I have a guess."

Nonna chuckled and continued on. "I'm at your Mama's. I decided to fly in for Thanksgiving and surprise you!" Olivia shrieked with excitement. It had been eleven months since Nonna had left and, although they talked most days, it wasn't the same as being together.

"Can we come over? Are you staying with Mama and Papa or with us? When did you get here? How long are you staying?" Olivia fired off questions so fast that Nonna didn't have time to answer until she took a breath.

"I am staying with your parents because I want to spend some time with your Mama. But I'll be here for two weeks, and you better get over here with my great-granddaughter in a hurry!" They hung up and Olivia packed a bag with snacks and a few toys for Joy. She finished up dishes and paced the floors until Joy woke up from her nap.

When Joy awoke, she set off for her Mama's house. Nonna met her at the door, and they hugged and hugged. Joy stared at Nonna shyly, but soon opened up when Nonna offered her some homemade chocolate chip cookies. Mama joined them, and they had a delightful visit laughing at Joy's antics and catching up.

Olivia promised to come by the next afternoon to make plans for Thanksgiving. They decided that she would host this year, and Nonna would stay a few nights with her and Brad to help with preparations. Brad's family would join them, too.

Olivia's cooking skills had grown by leaps and bounds, but she'd never hosted a holiday dinner. Lisa gave her a few of her tried and true recipes, and Nonna would help with the turkey and her famous stuffing. The night before everyone was set to arrive, she and Nonna arranged the tables and set them in her finest china. As they stood and admired their work, Olivia realized she'd gone several days without thinking of her loss. At first she felt guilty, but deep down knew it was progress.

The next day her house was bustling with family and filled with tantalizing aromas from the kitchen. Brad carved the turkey and B. G. led them in prayer. Mary and Nonna doted on Joy, Papa enjoyed chatting with the men, and even Mama seemed to have a good time. At one point, Mama put her hand on Olivia's shoulder and whispered, "The table looks really nice. You've become a good homemaker."

Olivia couldn't believe it. "Thank you, Mama." *And thank you, Lord, for hope in our relationship.*

After supper, B. G. encouraged them to share what they were thankful for this past year. As they took turns around the table, Olivia knew she wanted to thank them for their love and support while she and Brad dealt with their loss.

When it was her turn, Olivia cleared her throat and began to pour her heart out. "When David died, I thought I would die, too. I have never imagined such grief was possible. I can't even remember the first weeks after David's death. It was like I wasn't here."

She looked at Nonna. "You took care of Joy and my home while all I could do was breathe. You knew when to let me grieve and when it was time to hand the reins back over to me."

Next she turned to Papa B. G. and Nana Mary. "You sent me cards, called, prayed with me and loved me while I had nothing to give back." She put her hand tenderly on Mama's shoulder and said to her parents, "Mama, Papa, we've been through some hard times. I've worried you crazy with some of my decisions. But we have some better days ahead, and I love you both very much."

Next she gazed at Brad, and at this point she began to cry. "And you, my rock. You held me, cared for me, asked nothing from me, and gave me all of yourself even though you were grieving, too. Another man couldn't have handled what we've had to walk through. I'm so glad you're the one I get to spend the rest of my life with. I'm *most* thankful for you." Brad lifted her hand to his lips for a kiss.

Many wiped tears away and tapped on their glasses like at a wedding reception. Olivia's eyes were blurred with tears as she continued: "I thank God for walking through the valley of the shadow with me; for carrying me when I had no strength left to walk." She was thankful for moments like these when she could appreciate and enjoy life again.

That weekend, Brad and Olivia drove to the tree farm to cut down their Christmas tree – an established tradition by now. Joy loved the horses and helped pick out the tree. They found the fattest one in the lot. Back home, Olivia reminisced about the Christmas when she was alone, wishing she had someone to share the little things with. *Thank you, God, for answering that prayer in my life.*

On Christmas Eve, Brad and Olivia let Joy sleep with them so they could start Christmas morning with snuggles. Olivia's thoughts turned to David. *I wonder if he would have been walking by now and getting into everything. This bed might not have been big enough for the four of us.* She pushed the thought aside and led Joy to her stocking.

Once the holidays had passed, Olivia knew it was time to go see Doc and confirm what she already knew – she was pregnant. She had suspected since a little before Thanksgiving but was too scared to deal with the thought over the holidays. When she got to the office, Dr. B met her in the exam room and administered the test herself. While the results processed, she sat in the exam room with Olivia and talked about whatever came to mind. Olivia knew what Doc was doing, but appreciated her effort to lighten the mood.

The nurse knocked on the door and handed Doc the results.

"Well, Olivia, it's positive." Olivia didn't know how to respond. Part of her was elated, and part of her was terrified that something would happen again. Doc hugged her. "I know you're worried, Olivia. I would be lying if I said I'm not, too. But that won't do either of us any good. We're going to take one day at a time and try not to let fear set in."

Olivia nodded. "I know, Doc." She wiped a tear away. "I'm so scared."

When Doc realized how far along Olivia was, she decided to check to see if they could hear the heartbeat. While she rubbed the Doppler over Olivia's stomach, all they heard was static. "We're a tad early, Olivia, so if we don't hear it this time, we will next time for sure." She held the Doppler on a moment longer, and then the sound of the heartbeat came through.

"Oh!" Olivia gasped. "Do you hear that?!" Doc nodded and broke out in a grin.

Doc helped Olivia up and hugged her once again. "And now we pray."

Olivia drove straight to Brad's school to tell him. She couldn't wait another minute. He saw her in the door window and rushed out of his classroom, his face filled with alarm. Olivia reassured him nothing was wrong. "Can we go somewhere private for a few minutes?" she asked. Brad grabbed an office person to supervise his classroom, then led her to the conference room and shut the door. They sat at the table and she clasped his hand. "I'm pregnant, Brad."

He stared at her in disbelief. "Are you sure?"

"Yes, I saw Dr. B today. We heard the heartbeat!"

Brad was astonished. "I thought you couldn't hear that until you were further along."

"I'm about three months. I didn't want to tell you until I was past the first trimester. I've just been too scared to hope." There was no shrieking or twirling her in circles like when she was pregnant with David. They were both afraid to get excited. They agreed to keep the news to themselves as long as they could. They ended in prayer, pleading with God to protect this baby, to help it form as it should, and to bless them with a healthy and safe pregnancy. Olivia felt better after they prayed and left the office to pick up Joy from preschool.

Olivia and Lisa were baking and the kids were playing in the living room. Lindsey was in her high chair eating Cheerios. "How

Finding Hope

are you doing, Olivia? You're awful quiet lately. Is there something you want to talk about?"

They sat down while the pies baked, and Olivia decided to tell her she was expecting again. "What?!" Lisa exclaimed. "When did you find out?"

"I found out at the end of January."

"That was two months ago! I can't believe you've been keeping it to yourself that long!"

"I would've told you, but I'm so nervous. I'm trying not to get too excited in case something goes wrong."

"I understand, Olivia. So when are you due? July or August?"

Olivia shook her head. "No, I'm due June 10th."

"What? Girl, that's four months away! We have to plan a shower!" Olivia knew that Lisa would be excited.

"Lisa, let's take things slow. There's a chance that what happened with David was genetic and not random. I don't want to be unrealistic."

Lisa grabbed both of her hands. "Let's start praying, Olivia. Would you be open to sharing the news at Bible study? We need to get people praying!" Olivia wanted to talk it over with Brad first. She knew he wouldn't mind an announcement; he was more concerned about Olivia being *ready* to share.

That night they talked and decided it was time to start letting people know. Olivia would be showing soon, and they wanted to tell their family before they heard it through the grapevine. Olivia asked Lisa to keep it to herself until she had time to tell Mama and Papa and Brad's parents.

Later that night, once Joy was all tucked in, she decided to call Nonna.

She dialed the number and held her breath without realizing it. On the fourth ring Nonna answered. Olivia told her the news and waited for her response. "I've been praying you'd get pregnant again soon, Olivia. I am so happy for you. How are you doing?" They talked for hours, and Nonna understood Olivia's fear. She encouraged her to trust God. "We have to pray, honey. I will be praying night and day for this one. Is it okay if I share with my ladies Bible study group so they can pray, too?" Olivia agreed and they prayed before they hung up.

Mama and Papa didn't say much, but Mom and Dad Parks were encouraging. They got their church praying, too. Olivia thought this must be the most prayed for baby in the country. She tried to trust God, but spent many days agonizing over what she would do if something went wrong again.

Dr. B saw her more often than she had the other pregnancies. Olivia knew it was more for reassurance than anything. There wasn't much anyone could do but wait. The months seemed to crawl by, but they did pass. By the time she was a month away from her due date, Olivia was a wreck. The waiting and worrying was exhausting. She wanted to have the baby and know what the outcome would be for her family.

Brad tried not to show how nervous he was. He wanted to be strong for Olivia. He spent a lot of time outside because doing something physical helped his stress level. It still didn't make sense why they had to go through what they did, but he had come to peace with the fact that no one was promised a trouble-free life. He was thankful that he caught glimpses of happiness in Olivia. He knew, in time, that the waves of testing that had threatened to capsize their faith would turn back into calm seas.

He hoped that this pregnancy would be different; that this baby would be healthy. They didn't talk about it much. Olivia was too nervous, and he couldn't find the right words. Each day he walked into the school, Ben anxiously waited for some news. It seemed everyone they knew was ready for this little one to arrive.

At twelve days past her due date, labor began. Brad and Olivia dropped Joy off at Lisa's. They met Dr. B at the hospital, and she checked Olivia right away. "You're at three centimeters, but I'm going to keep you here since you're so far overdue. Why don't you go walk the halls for a while and see if you can get things to pick up a little."

Olivia and Brad walked and walked. Several hours later Doc checked her again. She had made a little more progress, but Doc sent her back out to walk more.

It felt like time was standing still while they waited, but labor finally progressed and soon it was time to push. Brad held Olivia's hand. Dr. Batten was at the foot of the bed and announced it was baby time.

The room was silent as the baby was born; no crying filled the air. Olivia didn't reach for her baby this time, and all eyes were on Dr. B. She cleared out the baby's mouth. Moments later, a soft cry filled the room. No one moved.

Dr. B blinked back tears. "It's a girl, Olivia. She looks perfect." It was the first time Olivia had ever seen her cheerful doctor cry. "Do you want to hold her?" Olivia shook her head no.

"Please have the pediatrician check her over. I have to know if she's okay." The minutes ticked by and Olivia worried herself sick. Brad slipped out to see what was taking so long. He walked back in with a huge grin.

The nurse was behind him with her sweet girl. "She's okay, Mommy." Olivia reached for her daughter, unaware of the tears that streamed down her cheeks. She held her close and thanked God as though they were the only ones in the room.

It's a girl. She's okay. She's beautiful. When Olivia composed herself, she and Brad sat together on the bed and marveled at their gift from God. They counted and recounted her fingers and toes. They traced her tiny lips with their fingers and rejoiced in the clear report on her health.

"Of all the names we've talked about, which one should we choose?" Olivia asked.

"Grace," Brad responded with confidence. Olivia nodded. It was perfect.

God had given them a gift, and he had shown his grace time and time again in her life. Through all the ups and downs, he had been there. Olivia was no longer so naive to think that she and Brad would live a life with no sorrow or trials. She was just thankful that God had provided the perfect man to walk beside her on this journey called life.

Elizabeth Diaz

The End

Thank you for reading my debut novel!
Please remember to spread the word about my book if you like it.
By using word-of-mouth, you help to bless an author.
Like – Share - Leave a review

- Elizabeth Diaz

Please join me online:

http://elizabethdiazauthor.com

Facebook:
http://www.facebook.com/ElizabethDiazAuthor

Twitter:
http://www.twitter.com/elizabe94279761

Keep checking online for the next book in the Generations of Hope series:
Choosing Joy

Made in the USA
Charleston, SC
13 February 2015